"You're obviously willing to play with fire," Pete said.

Was she? Ten minutes  that the opposite was take another emotiona had changed everythi

"Is that a problem?"

Pete stared at her for a very long time before a grin spread across his face. "Not for me."

"Okay, then, let me get started on dinner."

He hesitated then. "This is just about dinner, right?"

She wanted to throw caution completely to the wind and say no, that it was about seduction, but some lingering shred of common sense crept in. This was the man who'd almost destroyed her, after all.

"It's just about dinner," she confirmed.

Pete nodded. "Good to know."

Because he looked so sweet trying to hide his disappointment, she couldn't resist adding, "I'll let you know about dessert later."

Dear Reader,

June, the ideal month for weddings, is the perfect time to celebrate true love. And we are doing it in style here at Silhouette Special Edition as we celebrate the conclusion of several wonderful series. With *For the Love of Pete*, Sherryl Woods happily marries off the last of her ROSE COTTAGE SISTERS. It's Jo's turn this time—and she'd thought she'd gotten Pete Catlett out of her system for good. But at her childhood haven, anything can happen! Next, MONTANA MAVERICKS: GOLD RUSH GROOMS concludes with Cheryl St.John's *Million-Dollar Makeover*. We finally learn the identity of the true heir to the Queen of Hearts Mine—and no one is more shocked than the owner herself, the plain-Jane town… dog walker. When she finds herself in need of financial advice, she consults devastatingly handsome Riley Douglas—but she soon finds his influence exceeds the business sphere.…

And speaking of conclusions, Judy Duarte finishes off her BAYSIDE BACHELORS miniseries with *The Matchmakers' Daddy*, in which a wrongly imprisoned ex-con finds all kinds of second chances with a beautiful single mother and her adorable little girls. Next up in GOING HOME, Christine Flynn's heartwarming miniseries, is *The Sugar House*, in which a man who comes home to right a wrong finds himself falling for the woman who's always seen him as her adversary. Patricia McLinn's next book in her SOMETHING OLD, SOMETHING NEW… miniseries, *Baby Blues and Wedding Bells*, tells the story of a man who suddenly learns that his niece is really…his daughter. And in *The Secrets Between Them* by Nikki Benjamin, a divorced woman who's falling hard for her gardener learns that he is in reality an investigator hired by her ex-father-in-law to try to prove her an unfit mother.

So enjoy all those beautiful weddings, and be sure to come back next month! Here's hoping you catch the bouquet.…

Gail Chasan
Senior Editor

Please address questions and book requests to:
Silhouette Reader Service
U.S.: 3010 Walden Ave., P.O. Box 1325, Buffalo, NY 14269
Canadian: P.O. Box 609, Fort Erie, Ont. L2A 5X3

SHERRYL WOODS

For the Love of Pete

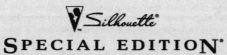

SPECIAL EDITION®

Published by Silhouette Books

America's Publisher of Contemporary Romance

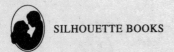 **SILHOUETTE BOOKS**

ISBN 0-373-24687-0

FOR THE LOVE OF PETE

SHERRYL WOODS

has written more than seventy-five novels. She also operates her own bookstore, Potomac Sunrise, in Colonial Beach, Virginia. If you can't visit Sherryl at her store, then be sure to drop her a note at P.O. Box 490326, Key Biscayne, FL 33149 or check out her Web site at www.sherrylwoods.com.

Dear Reader,

Of all the D'Angelo sisters, the youngest—Jo—is by far the most reluctant to run to Rose Cottage when her life falls apart. Jo knows firsthand just how powerful a pull this place by the Chesapeake Bay can have when it comes to love. She met her first love there…and had her heart broken.

But the D'Angelo women are a force to be reckoned with when they go into protective big-sister mode, and they want Jo where they can look out for her and help her to heal. And then they inadvertently deliver up the one man most likely to remind her of just how devastating love can be.

But this is Rose Cottage, after all, and it definitely has enough magic left to mend one more heart. In its cozy rooms, Jo remembers why she fell in love with Pete Catlett the first time, and he does everything in his power to see that she doesn't get away a second time.

I hope you've enjoyed sharing the enchantment of Rose Cottage and its effect on the D'Angelo sisters. The truth is, wherever we find love will forever be touched with magic in our memories.

All best,

Sheryl Woods

Prologue

"Pack your bags and come to Virginia," Ashley commanded the morning after Jo's life had been turned upside down by her lying, cheating ex-fiancé.

Jo sighed. She'd planned to spend the whole day in bed, licking her wounds in private, maybe eating the entire pint of Ben & Jerry's ice cream she had stashed in the freezer. Her funk had been interrupted before it could even get going by this call from all three of her sisters. She knew they were all on the line, even though Ashley was the only one who'd spoken so far. She could hear them breathing, while they left the coaxing to their big sister.

"How did you find out?" She thought she'd made it absolutely clear to their folks that her broken engagement was something she'd wanted to announce to her sisters herself…maybe next June, when the shock had worn off.

Unfortunately Max and Colleen D'Angelo weren't great at keeping quiet. They thought families should stick together in times of crisis. Her sisters had learned the lesson well. Until now, Jo had always found that comforting.

"Nothing stays secret in this family for long," Ashley responded, stating the obvious. "What I don't understand is why you didn't say something yourself. You should have called us the minute you caught James cheating."

"Why?" Jo grumbled. "So you could come up here and personally rip his heart out?" The image gave her a certain amount of bloodthirsty satisfaction, which she found deeply troubling. She liked to think of herself as kindhearted.

"That or some other part of his anatomy," Ashley said.

"That's precisely the reason I didn't call," Jo explained, shaking off the chill that had run down her spine at her sister's words. Ashley was perfectly capable of making good on such a threat. She had the protective big sister thing down pat. "I handled it in my own way. Besides, I didn't want all this sympathy, and I definitely don't want to run away. The humiliation of discovering James in bed with another woman was bad enough. I won't let him chase me off. My life is here in Boston. I'm not budging because of that scumbag."

In fact, this whole mess had reminded her of just how determined she was to make a life for herself in Boston. It had brought back way too many memories of another man she'd loved, another man who had cheated on her and forever ruined the love she'd once felt for Rose Cottage, her grandmother's home in Virginia. Even now, fresh as this was, she was having a hard time deciding which betrayal had been more devastating.

Worse, even though they'd never known about that earlier disaster, Jo had anticipated exactly how her sisters would react to this one. Though she sometimes thought of herself as the odd man out—the only one whose name wasn't somehow tied to *Gone With the Wind,* her Southern mother's favorite book—she'd known they would rally around her and insist that she come to Virginia, where they could fuss over her. The scene of that heart-breaking first betrayal was the last place on Earth she wanted to be—not that her sisters had any way of knowing that. She'd kept her own counsel back then and dealt with the anguish in private. Only her beloved grandmother had known the details, and she'd honored Jo's wishes never to discuss what had happened.

"You may as well give in and do this gracefully," Maggie chimed in on another extension, dismissing Jo's protests.

"Yes," Melanie added. "Don't make us come up to Boston to get you."

Jo's chuckle turned into a sob. It was too late to regret her part in insisting that each of her sisters go to Rose Cottage after their lives had fallen apart. How could she explain that it was different for her without divulging the secret she'd kept from them all these years? Then the fussing would really begin in earnest.

"I can't," she whispered. It was one thing for Ashley, Maggie and Melanie to make new lives for themselves in Virginia, but Rose Cottage was where Jo's heart had been broken the first time. How could she go there to heal now, when there were so many ghosts from the past to be faced in that place? Visiting for a day or two had been difficult enough. Staying any longer, risking a chance encounter with the man she'd once loved so deeply, would be torment.

"I'd like to know why not," Ashley demanded. "If you can't take the time off work, quit."

"Work's not the issue," Jo said miserably, though it didn't surprise her that it was the first thing her big sister had thought of. Even now, with her workaholic tendencies held in check by her new husband, Ashley was still driven.

"Then what is?" Ashley asked.

"I'm better off here," Jo said, knowing it was a weak response but unwilling to admit the truth. None of them knew how crazy in love she'd been during that last summer she'd spent at Rose Cottage. They'd all been busy with summer jobs back in Boston that year. She'd spent the entire summer alone with her grandmother…and with Pete.

She'd been so sure Pete Catlett was *the* one. She'd believed him when he said he loved her, believed it enough to make love with him, believed it well enough when he'd promised to be waiting when she returned the following year.

But even before the last of the autumn leaves had fallen, her grandmother had casually mentioned that Pete had gotten married. A few months later, there had been mention of a baby, too. A boy.

She and her grandmother had both maintained the pretense that Cornelia Lindsay was doing little more than passing along local gossip about an acquaintance, but Jo had heard the compassion underlying the words, the awareness that what she was telling Jo would devastate her.

Jo had felt utterly betrayed, especially because the young man she'd loved and trusted hadn't even had the courage to tell her himself. Not that that would have made the pain any easier to bear, but it would have reassured her that she hadn't misjudged him entirely, that she had mattered to him, at least for a time.

It had taken her years to find the courage to risk her heart again, and just look what had happened, the same damn thing…or something that felt a whole lot like it.

No, Virginia was definitely not the place for her. She needed to stay right here in Boston and bury herself in work. She liked her job as a landscape designer. She had her friends, even if none of them were as close as the sisters who were insisting she come to Rose Cottage so they could hover over her.

"I can't come to Virginia," she said again, her tone flat and, she hoped, unequivocal.

Melanie heaved an exaggerated sigh. "I guess that means we leave in the morning, right, Ash and Maggie?"

"I can be ready by 5:00 a.m.," Ashley said. "How about the rest of you?"

"Absolutely," Melanie responded.

"Guys!" Jo protested with what she knew was wasted breath. They weren't going to be satisfied until they'd seen her for themselves, babied her for a few days or weeks. It was the curse of being the youngest that they thought she needed extra care at a time like this.

"You can stop us," Ashley reminded her. "All you

have to do is agree to come quietly. Settle in for the winter, Jo. It'll be peaceful and quiet. We won't bug you unless you want us to."

"That's a joke. You're already bugging me," Jo pointed out.

"Yes, but with the best intentions," Melanie said cheerfully.

"Let me see what I can work out," Jo said finally. "Maybe I'll come for the weekend so you can see that I'm not a complete basket case. James isn't worth falling apart over."

She figured she could hide the truth about her aversion to Rose Cottage for a couple of days, then scamper straight back to Boston. In fact, two days seemed safe enough, however she looked at it. After all, she hadn't run into Pete on any of her previous brief visits. She'd been very careful not to spend too much time in public.

Though her reluctance to go places had clearly aroused her sisters' suspicions, they'd never called her on it with more than the most cursory questions. Any hesitation she showed now, they would blame on her broken heart. They'd never guess it had anything at all to do with a long-ago relationship that had ended badly and a panicky fear that she would encounter Pete Catlett again.

Not that her self-imposed isolation had worked all that well when it came to her own feelings. She'd been aware of Pete every second of every visit. Just driving to Rose Cottage, she'd seen his name on construction jobs all over in the small waterfront towns of White Stone and Irvington. Knowing that he had built a reputation for himself doing what he loved had only stirred mixed emotions. She wished she were a big enough person to be happy for him, but a part of her had seen that success as further evidence of betrayal. She was the one who'd encouraged him to fight for his dream, despite his mother's insistence that he attend college instead. Now he'd achieved that dream with some other woman by his side.

"A weekend won't cut it," Melanie said firmly. "We made Ashley come for three weeks. If Ms. Workaholic could do that, you ought to be able to commit for at least a month, minimum."

"Right," Ashley agreed. "Besides, you work for a landscape company. How much work do you do in winter, anyway? And if you get the itch to design something, I'll bet Mike can put you to work. He has more landscaping jobs than he can handle these days."

"You worked all of this out before you called, didn't you?" Jo said, increasingly resigned to her fate. "You even have Mike in on it. Does he know you're now hiring employees for him, Ashley?"

"Of course," Ashley said. "I never go into a courtroom or into an argument with you unprepared. Besides, this was Mike's idea, right, Melanie?"

"Absolutely," Melanie said, speaking for her husband. "He really is swamped, Jo. You'd be doing him— and me—a favor. I'd like to see a whole lot more of my husband than I do. Come on, Jo, say yes."

Jo sighed.

"Call us when you're a couple of hours away," Maggie said, obviously convinced that they'd won. "We'll get a fire going and some dinner on the table. Rose Cot-

tage is a wonderful place for you to be. It certainly did
the trick for the rest of us. I can't think of anything co-
zier than sitting in front of a fire and letting all your
cares drift away while the snow falls outside."

"It snows in Boston," she reminded them, making one
last halfhearted attempt to put them off. "I hate snow."

"You do not," Melanie protested. "Besides, it's common there. It's so rare here that it's magical. Just wait.
Maybe you'll follow tradition and meet the man of your
dreams here, too."

"Whatever," Jo said, seeing little sense in trying to
shake their faith in the cottage's magical properties
when it came to romance.

In her current mood, however, she couldn't imagine
that there was enough magic on Earth, much less at
Rose Cottage, to make her feel one bit better, not about
snow, and definitely not about love.

The irony, of course, was that she was the first of the
D'Angelo sisters to find the right man at Rose Cottage.
She wondered what they'd think of the tradition if they
knew how badly that had ended.

Chapter One

As if to prove her sisters' point, snow had started falling an hour after Jo's arrival at Rose Cottage. She stared out the window as the big, wet flakes landed on the ground. With some effort, she bit back an hysterical sob.

"What?" Ashley asked, coming up to slide a comforting arm around her shoulders.

Jo turned to her big sister, her eyes stinging with tears. "Do you guys have to be right about everything?" she asked in frustration.

Ashley grinned. "Pretty much. Why?"

"The snow's started right on cue. Surely you don't actually control the weather."

Hearing that, Melanie and Maggie rushed over to join them.

"It's going to be beautiful," Melanie promised, stepping up beside her and circling an arm around Jo's waist. "You'll see. By morning it will be like a winter wonderland out there."

"And I'll be trapped in here all by myself," Jo grumbled, awash in an unbecoming and uncommon sea of self-pity. "I'll have nothing to do but think." She shuddered at the prospect. Her thoughts were not all that happy these days. She didn't want to be alone with them.

"We'll rescue you," Ashley promised.

"I'll bring Jessie by and the two of you can go sledding," Melanie suggested, referring to her energetic stepdaughter. "That'll put some color in your cheeks."

"It's cold out there."

"Please," Melanie commented. "Compared to Boston, this is practically tropical. Besides, you used to love sledding."

"When I was eight," Jo muttered.

"Okay, if that doesn't appeal to you, we can all sit here in front of the fire and drink hot chocolate and eat s'mores," Ashley said, her tone soothing, as if she sensed that Jo was about to come unglued on them. "Or Maggie can bake. The whole house will fill up with all these wonderful scents, just the way it did at home when Mom made us cookies on snowy days."

Jo knew they would all be on her doorstep first thing in the morning tomorrow and every day after, unless she put a stop to it right this second. If she ate as many cookies as Maggie was likely to bake, she'd be a blimp by spring.

"Okay, enough," she said firmly. "Don't listen to all my grumbling. You can't turn your lives upside down for me. I appreciate your concern, but I'll be fine. If my thoughts start getting too dark and dreary, I can always go for a walk."

"Of course you can. And there are a few things around this place that need to be taken care of," Ashley said briskly. "Since I was the last one here, I'll make a list of the stuff I never got to do. In fact, I'll make a couple of calls first thing tomorrow and try to line up the right people to come by. You'll just have to be here when they show up."

"I can't afford to spend a fortune on repairs," Jo reminded her. "Until Mike needs me for something, I'm on an unpaid leave of absence. My boss was generous in agreeing to keep the job open for me."

"Generous, my ass," Ashley retorted. "You're the most talented person he has."

Jo grinned at her. "Thanks, big sister, but you're not only biased, you don't know a thing about landscape design."

"But Mike does," Melanie chimed in. "And he says you're good. Don't worry about money, Jo. You'll have all the work you want while you're here. You just have to speak up whenever you're ready."

"And in the meantime, don't worry about the repair bills," Ashley said. "We've pooled money to get this place fixed up. Melanie got the rooms painted and worked on the garden, Maggie made improvements in the kitchen." She shrugged. "I didn't do much, since Josh was teaching me to relax, so I've chipped in for the work that still needs to be done. All the bills will come to me. You'll just need to supervise."

Jo regarded them with bemusement. "Why waste any more money on this place? You all have your own homes now, and Mom hasn't been here since Grand-mother died except to see you. Why spend a fortune to fix up Rose Cottage?"

"It's not a fortune. We've all agreed Rose Cottage needs to stay in the family, which means it's sensible to keep it in good repair," Ashley said. "And it's yours for as long as you want it."

"Thanks," Jo said, her voice choked. Until she'd ac-tually gotten here, she hadn't realized how much she missed her big sisters. Right this second, it didn't even matter that they were gathered around her in Rose Cot-tage, the site of her first painful love affair. "You guys are the best." She sniffed and brushed away a traitorous tear.

"Don't start bawling now," Maggie scolded, handing her a tissue. "Or we'll have to stick around till you're finished and we'll wind up being snowed in. Much as you love us right this second, I doubt you're up for a slumber party."

Jo forced a misty-eyed smile. "True." The last thing she wanted was to give her sisters too much time to cross-examine her. "Go, while you can. And call me when you get home, so I won't worry that you've skid-ded off the road and landed in a ditch."

Relieved by their acquiescence, she stood in the doorway watching until they were out of sight, then sighed heavily. The ground was almost covered with snow already, and there was no sign that it was stopping. It was a little like a winter wonderland, she admitted as she stared toward the Chesapeake Bay.

Once, when she'd been starry-eyed and in love, she had thought this would be the place she'd spend the rest of her life. Now it felt more like a beautiful prison.

At least she could leave it when it got to be too much, she reminded herself. If she managed to plaster a cheery smile on her face each time she saw her sisters, eventually they'd relent and let her go home. Until then, she'd lay low and pretend that she'd never even heard of Pete Catlett, much less loved him enough to let him break her heart.

Pete's answering service relayed the message that there were some loose and rotting boards on the porch at Rose Cottage, along with a plea that he get to them first thing in the morning if at all possible. The service hadn't said who'd called, though his guess was Ashley.

Damn, he thought, his mind immediately going back seven years to the summer when Rose Cottage had been like a second home to him. Maybe even more like the first real home he'd known. Mrs. Lindsay had had a soothing temperament, especially compared to his mother's quick flashes of irritation.

And, of course, there had been Jo with her huge blue eyes, scattering of freckles dusted across a pert nose and a mouth that had tempted him from the first time he'd seen those lush lips curve into a shy smile.

They had shared so many hopes and dreams that summer. He'd been so sure that in a few years they'd find a way to be together forever. He'd made a lot of promises that he'd had every intention of keeping.

Then he'd made one stupid, idiotic mistake in the first weeks after Jo had gone back to Boston, and his life had been sent in another direction entirely.

He'd wanted to blame Kelsey Prescott for getting pregnant, but the one thing he'd vowed to do the moment his father abandoned him and his mom was to be responsible. He'd sworn he would never walk out on a child of his, not even if he wasn't in love with the child's mother. He'd find some way to make it work. In his head, if not his heart, he'd accepted that he was every bit as responsible for that baby's creation as Kelsey was.

And he'd tried doing the right thing. Lord knows, he'd tried. But Kelsey had felt trapped and angry from the very beginning. She couldn't seem to let go of her bitterness the way Pete had tried valiantly to do. Nothing Pete had done could make up for the fact that she'd had to give up her dream of moving away to someplace more exciting than the rural area where they'd both grown up.

For five years, he'd fought a losing battle to keep her and his son, but now she and Davey were living in Richmond and Pete hardly ever saw his boy, except for the occasional weekend or holiday visits or a few bittersweet weeks each summer. In the end, things had turned out exactly the way he'd sworn they wouldn't, with him separated from his son. Had he been able to see into the future, maybe he would have done things differently. Maybe he and Jo could have found some way to work past the stupid mistake he'd made and the two of them could have been there for his son, giving him the kind of stable family he certainly didn't have now.

As it was, Pete had never had the courage to face Jo. He'd known she would never understand how he could claim to love her, then have sex with someone else a few weeks after she'd gone. Hell, he didn't entirely understand it himself, except that he'd been young and stupid and living in the moment. At twenty, he'd been more attuned to his hormones than his brain. He'd actually tried explaining that to Jo's grandmother, but even though Cornelia Lindsay hadn't said a single harsh or accusing word, the disappointment in her eyes had only compounded his sense of shame. He couldn't bear the prospect of seeing that same disappointment in Jo's eyes, so he'd stayed silent and let others break her heart with the news.

Over the last year, he'd seen people coming and going at Rose Cottage. He knew that, one by one, Jo's sisters had come there, fallen in love and married. All were now living in the area, but he hadn't caught the first glimpse of Jo.

Feeling awkward and ill at ease the whole time, he'd even done some work for Ashley and her new husband, Josh Madison, but the subject of Jo had never even come up, eventually convincing him that Ashley didn't know about the betrayal. As clannish as they were, he'd supposed they all hated him on Jo's behalf. It had been a relief, in a way, to know that she'd kept silent, though it worried him some that she apparently hadn't even turned to those closest to her back then. Still, his guilt ran deep.

Even after that reassuring encounter with Ashley several weeks back, he dismissed the message he'd received this morning. He told himself it was because he was swamped with work. Now, though, he had no more excuses. On his way home, he ignored the churning in his gut and drove to Rose Cottage to take a look at what needed to be done.

Snow still clung to the trees and lay several inches deep on the front steps. Even though the snow was undisturbed by footprints, there was smoke curling from the chimney. A light was burning in the living room, and another shone brightly in the kitchen.

Pete sat in his car and debated whether he ought to drive right on. He wasn't sure he was ready to face any of the D'Angelo women, not at Rose Cottage. He'd only been able to work for Ashley because the job had been at Josh's home. He knew that stepping through this door would strip away the scab on an old wound.

"Don't be an idiot," he finally muttered. It was a job. No big deal. They'd probably rented the place to some stranger. There was nothing here to be afraid of. Chiding himself for his cowardice, he strode to the front door and knocked.

When the door swung open, he wasn't sure who was more stunned, him or the pale woman who stared at him with sad, haunted eyes.

"What are you doing here?" he and Jo said in a chorus.

He tried for a smile. "Sorry. I had a call to come by about some needed repairs. I had no idea you were here. Frankly, I can't believe you called me."

She regarded him with bewilderment. "I didn't. What repairs? Ashley said something about making a few calls, but I had no idea she'd done it. We never even went over her list of what needs to be done."

"Whoever called said something about some loose and rotting boards on the porch."

"It was dark when I got here. I didn't notice."

"You just arrived, then?"

She shook her head. "Last night, actually."

"And you haven't been out all day," he said.

She regarded him with suspicion. "How do you know that?" she asked, a surprisingly defensive note in her voice.

"Settle down, darlin'. Nobody's been tattling on you, at least not to me." He gestured toward the steps. "The only footprints out here are mine."

Her temper deflated at once. "Sorry," she said stiffly.

He hesitated, then forced himself to ask, "Would you prefer I send someone else over to check out the porch? I could have someone come by in the morning. Your sister obviously didn't know that calling me would be a problem."

Indecision was written all over her face. She looked so lost, so thoroughly miserable, that Pete wanted to haul her into his arms and comfort her, but he no longer had that right. Once she would have slapped him silly if he'd tried, but something told him that whatever had sent her fleeing to Rose Cottage had wiped away that feistiness and strength.

"No," she said at last. "You're here. I don't want to try to explain to Ashley why I sent you away. I'll flip on the light so you can take a closer look."

Pete nodded. "Thanks."

A moment later, the light came on, and then the door firmly shut. He tried not to feel hurt at being so plainly dismissed and locked out, but he couldn't help it. Once he'd been warmly welcomed in this home. Once he'd been joyously welcomed by this woman. Having that door close quietly in his face was as effective as any slap. The message was just as clear: Jo would tolerate his presence as long as there was a job to do, but she wanted no further contact with him. Her reaction was only what he deserved, yet it rankled.

He spent a few minutes surveying the porch, determined that it needed to be totally replaced since half measures would only delay the inevitable. He made a few rough calculations on the notepad he always kept in his pocket, then knocked on the door again.

It took a long time for Jo to answer, and when she did, it was obvious she'd been crying. Her pale skin was streaked with tears. Pete's heart turned over at the sight.

"What?" she asked impatiently.

Forgetting all about the porch for the moment, he asked, "Jo, are you okay?"

"Nothing a little time won't cure," she said. "Or so they say. Personally, I think that's a crock."

He heard the unmistakable bitterness in her voice and concluded she was referring to something recent, though it could just as easily have had something to do with his betrayal all those years ago and a wound he'd caused that had yet to heal.

He shoved his hands in his pockets and risked another rejection. "Want to talk about it?"

"No, and certainly not with you," she said flatly. "What I want is to be left alone."

He knew he should take her at her word, but how could he? She looked as if she were on the verge of collapse. What were her sisters thinking, leaving her alone like this? Ignoring her words, he brushed right past her and walked inside the cottage, determined not to go until there was more color in her cheeks, even if anger at his presumption was what put it there.

It was like coming home. The paint was fresh and there were a few unfamiliar touches, but essentially it had hardly changed from the way he remembered it. It was warm and cozy with the fire blazing, the chairs covered with a cheery chintz fabric, the walls decorated with delicate watercolors of the Chesapeake Bay and one or two of the garden right here at Rose Cottage. Jo's grandmother had painted them. What they lacked in expertise, they made up for in sentiment.

"Have you eaten?" he asked briskly, heading for the kitchen as if he had a perfect right to do so. "I haven't and I'm starved."

Jo hurried to catch up with him, then faced him with a stubborn jut to her chin. "What is *wrong* with you?" she demanded. "You can't barge in here and take over, Pete."

"I just did, sweetheart. How about some soup?" he asked cheerfully, opening a cupboard to find it fully stocked with everything from chicken noodle to tomato soup. "Seems like the right kind of night for it. It's cold and raw outside."

The suggestion was greeted with silence. He took that as a good sign.

"Tomato soup and grilled cheese sandwiches," he decided, after checking out the contents of the fridge. "Your grandmother used to fix that for us all the time. Is it still your favorite?"

"I'm not hungry, and you need to go," Jo insisted, trying to reach around him to shut the cabinet door without actually touching him.

"I have time," he said, deliberately misinterpreting her objection and making it impossible for her to succeed in thwarting his actions. "Sit down. I'll have it ready in no time."

He began assembling the ingredients for their makeshift dinner with quick, efficient movements, finding pans where they'd always been, bowls and plates in the same cupboard. He was pretty sure the flower-trimmed plates had the same chips he remembered.

"Ah, you've already boiled water," he said, noting that the teakettle on the stove was still hot to the touch. "Teabags in the same place?"

He didn't wait for a response, just kept on making the meal, flipping the sandwiches as the bread turned a golden brown, stirring the soup. This was Davey's favorite meal, too, so Pete had become something of an expert.

He took heart from the fact that Jo hadn't blown up and insisted that he go. At the same time, it was telling that she apparently didn't have the strength to fight his obviously unwanted presence. Eventually, she simply sighed and sat down.

"So, what brings you to Rose Cottage?" he asked as he set the soup and sandwich in front of her.

She stared at the food, then scowled at him. "I don't want this and I don't want to make small talk, especially not with you," she said with a bit more spirit.

"I get that," he said. "But the food's hot and I'm here, so why not make the best of it?"

She frowned. "Were you always this annoying?"

"Probably," he admitted. "You tended to see the good in people. You probably overlooked it."

"Must have," she muttered, but she picked up her spoon and tasted the soup.

Pete felt a small sense of triumph when she swallowed the first spoonful, then went back for more. When she picked up her sandwich, he did a little mental tap dance. The food—or her annoyance with him—was putting a little color back into her cheeks. She didn't look nearly as sad and defeated as she had when he'd first arrived. He would have put up with a lot worse than what she'd dished out to see that change in her.

When she finally glanced his way, she asked suspiciously, "Who really called you to come by here? Are you sure you didn't make the whole thing up?"

He shrugged. "I can't say for certain who called. The answering service took the message. You said Ashley had told you she was going to call someone, so I assume it was her."

"But you?" she asked skeptically.

He grinned. "My number's in the book, so why not me? Besides, I did some work for her and Josh a while back. They were happy with it. Unless you filled her head with a list of all my shortcomings since then, it makes perfect sense."

"I've never even mentioned your name to her."

"Then what's the big deal?"

"I think you know the answer to that."

"It's a coincidence, Jo, not some big, diabolical conspiracy I worked out with your sister. Trust me, I have more than enough work to keep me busy—I don't need to drop in on unsuspecting people and beg for little nuisance jobs like this. I got a call. I came by to check things out. That's it. Till I saw the lights and the smoke coming from the chimney, I had no clue anyone was staying here."

"Okay, so you're just following up on a call," she finally conceded. "You've done your duty. Leave your estimate. I'll get another one. You'll lose."

"I don't think so," he said. What he'd said was true—this was a nothing little job for him, but he intended to do it. In fact, he was going to stick to Jo like glue till he found out why she'd looked like death warmed over when he'd turned up. "Whoever called was right. The porch is a disaster. Better to rip it off and start from scratch before someone gets hurt."

"Fine, but I'm sure someone else can do it cheaper," she said flatly. "Heck, I could probably do the work myself if I put my mind to it."

He grinned at that. "Really? You think so?"

"How hard could it be to nail a few boards together?" she said brashly. "And I wouldn't be charging Ashley some exorbitant price for labor."

"You haven't seen my estimate yet," he reminded her, not even trying to hide his amusement at her obvious ploy to get rid of him. "You just don't want me hanging around."

She met his gaze, then looked away, the color in her cheeks deepening. "No," she said softly, then immediately apologized. "Sorry."

"No offense taken," he said easily. "I could have someone else come by, but whoever called asked specifically for me. When loyal customers do that, I do the work. It's a point of honor."

She frowned at him. "As if," she said bitterly.

Her comment was like a slap. It stung. "I suppose I deserved that," he admitted.

"And more," she retorted. "Look, Pete, you can forget that whole trumped-up honor thing. I'll deal with my sisters. Besides, I thought you were building all these huge homes around here. Why would you want to waste time fixing up a porch?"

"Keeps me humble," he said lightly, though what he

wanted to say was that it would give him a chance to be around her again, to maybe make amends for what he'd done to her seven years ago. Now that he'd actually seen Jo again, he knew that all those feelings he'd tamped down so that he could stay married to Kelsey were as strong as ever.

"It's a bad idea," she said, half to herself.

"Why?" he asked, though he knew perfectly well precisely why she would see it that way. Seeing her had shot his defenses to hell, too.

She skewered him with a disbelieving look.

"Okay, scratch that. You're still furious with me. Can't say I blame you. What I did to you was inexcusable."

"You're wrong," she said fiercely. "I don't feel anything at all where you're concerned. Seven years is a long time, Pete. What we had is so over."

It was a blatant lie. Pete could see that in her stormy eyes, which was why he decided there was no way in hell he was backing off on doing this job, no matter how hard she fought him.

"Then having me underfoot won't bother you at all," he said pleasantly.

"Why are you doing this?" she asked plaintively.

He ignored the question. He figured she already knew the answer. She just wasn't ready to acknowledge it yet.

"I'll be by around eight," he said decisively. "Hope you weren't planning to sleep late. I'm going to be noisy, and I could use a cup of coffee when I get here. Mine's lousy, but I seem to recall you brewed the strong stuff."

He decided he'd done what he could for tonight, declared his intentions as plainly as he could, gotten her blood to pumping in the only way he knew how short of kissing her. He got to his feet.

"'Night, darlin'. Good to see you." He dropped a kiss on her already overheated cheek and tried not to notice that she was sputtering with indignation as he left.

In fact, as he crossed the lawn, she uttered a few words he'd never even realized she knew. They weren't complimentary.

Even with those words echoing in his head as he climbed into his car, he caught himself whistling happily. Whatever was going on with Jo that had brought her scurrying to the safe haven of Rose Cottage, he intended to see that he was there to help her through it. Last time she'd been hurt, he'd been the cause. This time, he would be the solution.

And when all was said and done, when fences were finally mended, who knew what might happen next?

Chapter Two

Of all the arrogant, annoying, impossible men on the face of the planet, how had Ashley somehow managed to come up with the one guaranteed to drive Jo insane? For a normally calm, placid individual, she'd used more curse words at top volume in the ten minutes following Pete's visit than she had in her entire lifetime. He'd apparently heard a few of them cross her lips, too, and they'd only made him laugh. The sound had reached her and, if anything, had only made her more furious. The man was absolutely insufferable. She definitely hadn't recalled that about him. It might have made things easier for her.

How dare he barge into Rose Cottage as if he had every right to be there? How dare he take over as if she were some basket case he didn't dare leave alone? Okay, so maybe she had looked a little pitiful when he'd first arrived, but that definitely wouldn't happen again. In the morning, she'd be ready for him. Too bad her grandmother had never kept a shotgun on the premises. Maybe waving one of those in his direction would convince him to leave her the hell alone.

She sighed as her flash of temper died. If that was what she really wanted.

The truth was her stupid heart had raced when she'd first glimpsed Pete on the porch. She could deny it till the cows came home, but on some level she'd been glad to see him. In fact, she'd shut the front door so securely to keep him from seeing any telltale reaction on her face. Or maybe just to prevent herself from flying straight into his powerful arms. On some primal level, that was exactly what she'd wanted to do. How idiotic was that? One glimpse of the man, and in five seconds her self-control and her good sense had been wrecked.

And that was before he'd ignored all her protests and barged in. After that, she hadn't had to fake her indignation. It took a lot of nerve for a man who'd all but destroyed her to walk inside her home and act as if nothing had happened, as if he belonged there. If he thought that half-assed acknowledgment that he'd mistreated her seven years ago was an acceptable apology, he was seriously mistaken. It was going to take more than a few pitiful words to win her forgiveness. She was going to make him work for it.

Now, unfortunately, it seemed that he was going to have plenty of time to come up with all the pretty words she needed to hear. He was going to be underfoot for who knew how long, and there wasn't a blessed thing she could do about it except stay as far away from Rose Cottage during the day as she possibly could.

As he'd probably guessed, firing him was not an option. It would only stir up more questions than she was prepared to answer. And perverse as he was, he'd probably see it as an admission that she was still attracted to him.

Which she was, dammit!

Her plan of action, such as it was, decided, Jo went to bed and tried to forget about how good Pete had looked in his snug, faded jeans and dark green sweater. Seven years had only made him more handsome. His face looked stronger and sexier with a day's stubble of beard shadowing his cheeks, and there was even more mischief in his dark eyes. Hell, the man radiated sex from every pore, which was something she had no business thinking about a married man, especially not a married man who'd broken her heart.

Come to think of it, for a married man he'd been awfully carefree about hanging out with her for a couple of hours when he should have been home with his wife and son. Obviously, his morals hadn't improved since the days when he'd slept with another woman shortly after professing his undying love for her. That alone should be warning enough for her to give him a very wide berth.

Because of that, she set the alarm for six. She'd be showered, dressed and on her way somewhere by seven, long before Pete showed up in the morning. It was one thing to agree to let him do the job Ashley had hired him to do. It was another thing entirely to stick around and watch and be tormented—and tempted—in the process.

* * *

Pete knew exactly how Jo's mind worked, which was one reason he was pulling up in front of Rose Cottage shortly after six-thirty in the morning. The fact that every light in the house was blazing told him he'd been right to guess that she would be preparing to be long gone before he turned up.

He sat in his truck with the heater pumped up on high and waited. Sure enough, at seven o'clock the lights began to switch off. Immediately after the last one went out, the front door opened. She was so busy concentrating on getting her key into the lock, she apparently didn't even notice when he cut the truck's engine, swung down from the front seat and stepped into her path. She turned around and ran smack into him. He steadied her and looked straight into eyes blazing with anger and dismay.

"Going somewhere?" he inquired, regarding her with amusement. "I don't recall you being such an early bird."

She frowned at him. "Why are you here?" she asked, guilt written all over her face.

"I told you I'd be here first thing this morning."

"You said eight o'clock."

"I did," he agreed. "And then I got to thinking."

Her gaze narrowed. "About what?"

"How likely it was that you'd bolt before I got here, if you had the chance."

"Maybe I was just going out to grab breakfast," she said defensively. "Maybe I'd planned to be back by eight."

"Did you?"

She avoided his gaze, apparently unwilling to utter a blatant lie. "Why does it even matter where I was going? You don't need me here. I'm sure you're perfectly capable of handling this very difficult job all by yourself."

"True, but I was counting on that coffee," he said cheerfully.

"I didn't make any coffee."

"Not a problem," he said, circling an arm around her shoulders and turning her in the direction of his truck. "Since I got such an early start, there's plenty of time for us to go into town and have breakfast together. I'll even treat."

"I am not going into town with you," she said, sounding horrified by the suggestion.

"Why not?"

"Because I'm not. It's a terrible idea. What on earth is wrong with you?"

Pete couldn't imagine why she found the idea so abhorrent. He concluded, though, that asking wasn't likely to get him a straight answer. "Then I'd say we're at an impasse," he said with a shrug. "Everyone knows it's vitally important to have coffee for the men on a job site. It's like an unwritten rule."

Her scowl deepened, but she whirled around and headed for the house. "Fine. I'll make your damn coffee, but then I'm leaving."

He beamed at her. "Works for me," he said.

Inside, though, he opened the refrigerator and took out eggs, bacon and butter. "Might as well have breakfast while we're at it."

Her color was definitely better this morning, but she still had that sad, haunted look in her eyes, and she was too damned thin. Whatever was bothering her had evidently ruined her appetite. He was no gourmet chef, as he'd heard her sister Maggie was, but he could handle breakfast.

"What makes you think I wasn't planning on meeting my sisters for breakfast in town?" she inquired testily.

"For one thing, you didn't mention it," he said reasonably. He leveled a look straight into her eyes. "Were you?"

Her gaze wavered before she finally sighed. "No."

"Then have a seat. I'll whip something up in no time. We can catch up."

"Pete, I don't want to catch up with you," she said with evident frustration. "I don't want to talk to you. I don't want to see you."

He shook his head. "Is that anything to say to an old friend?"

"You are not my friend."

He met her gaze. "I was. I could be again."

"I don't think so." Her anxious gaze settled on the coffeemaker as if she could will it to brew the coffee faster. "As soon as this is ready, I'm out of here. In fact, since it pretty much does the work all on its own, I'll go now. Help yourself when it's ready. Enjoy your breakfast."

When she reached for her coat, Pete put his hand on hers. She jerked away.

"Stop it," she ordered fiercely. "I don't want you touching me."

He winced at the evidence of her aversion. Okay, so he understood it, but that didn't mean it didn't cut right through him.

"Jo, come on," he pleaded. "We obviously need to talk. We need to settle a few things."

She glowered at him. "We needed to talk seven years ago, but I didn't see you beating down the door to do it."

Another direct hit, he thought wearily. She was getting good at it. "I was twenty years old and stupid. I should have talked to you, but you'd already left town."

"And what? The phones didn't work?"

"I was embarrassed and ashamed."

She gave him a disbelieving look.

"Okay, I was a coward," he admitted. "I came by and talked to your grandmother. That was hard enough. I didn't have the guts to face you. I figured she'd tell you everything. I convinced myself it would be easier for you to hear it from her."

"Of course you did," Jo accused bitterly. "And believe me, it was so much easier having my grandmother be the one to share the news that was going to break my heart," she added in a voice rich with sarcasm. "She tried hard to be nonchalant. So did I, but we were both lousy at it."

Pete winced at the image she'd painted. "I'm sorry," he said. "It was a rotten thing to do to you and to her."

"Yes, it was," she said, not giving an inch. "Now if we've rehashed the past sufficiently, do you mind if I take off?"

He made one last try to keep her there. "Sure you don't want to stay? I make a terrific omelet."

"So do a lot of people. It's not that hard." She gave him a withering look. "I trust I won't find you here when I get back."

His own appetite ruined, Pete put the food back in the refrigerator, then turned to face her. "I suppose that depends on how long you intend to hide out."

"As long as it takes."

She would do it, too. Pete could see in her eyes that she would find some way to avoid him until the job was done. Maybe he should let her, but he couldn't imagine himself giving up so easily. If she wanted him to pay penance for what he'd done to her, that was only fair. If she wanted to rail at him, curse him, keep him at arm's length, that was okay, too. He deserved whatever she wanted to dish out.

But he would keep coming back, not because he was stubborn. Not because he wanted to be a thorn in her side. He'd keep coming back because the moment he'd laid eyes on her again, he'd known he had no choice.

He was still in love with her, or at least with the sweet, vulnerable girl she'd once been. It remained to be seen if the woman was as captivating. Based on the way his hormones were raging, he was pretty sure she was.

Jo knew she wasn't thinking straight when she drove straight out to Maggie's farm, her temper still boiling. What was it going to take to make Pete see that she wanted absolutely nothing to do with him? She didn't want him as a friend. She certainly didn't want him as anything more. What did it say about him—or her—that he even thought she might? The man was married, for goodness sake, though he apparently didn't seem to care much about that little detail.

If she'd spent one more second with him at Rose Cottage, she might have slapped him silly for his presumption.

Or she might have kissed him. That had been a definite possibility, too. She was willing to admit that. She was such an idiot! Maybe she'd sunk so low that her morals were no better than his.

Before getting on the road, she'd spent a long time in the driveway thinking about that, shocked that she would even consider such a thing for a single second.

When he'd walked out of the house while she was still sitting there, her gaze had fallen on him with seven years of pent-up longing. She knew he was aware of her, knew he was counting on her staring when he hefted that heavy ax over his head and started his demolition of the porch.

Her hand was shaking so bad, she almost hadn't been able to turn the key in the ignition. She'd actually stalled out twice before she finally got away from Rose Cottage and Pete's barely muffled laughter. He hadn't even tried to hide his gloating.

All the way to Maggie's she kept telling herself to calm down. If her sister saw her like this, she would know something was up. It didn't take a genius to see that Pete had rattled her. Since she was never, ever rattled, it was going to be a dead giveaway.

When she pulled up outside of Maggie's, she spotted Ashley's and Melanie's cars. She cursed another blue streak at the sight and almost turned right around and headed back to town, but with all this adrenaline pumping, she was hungry. She cut the engine, drew in a deep calming breath and went inside.

She'd barely stepped into Maggie's gourmet, professional kitchen before her temper stirred again. All three women were seated at the table, the last crumbs of a pecan coffee cake on their plates, mugs filled with fragrant coffee. They looked so blasted innocent, but one of them was a traitor, albeit an unwitting one. Her money was definitely on Ashley. Jo figured she'd ask anyway, just in case she and Pete both had gotten it all wrong.

"Okay, which one of you did it?" she asked before she'd even removed her coat.

"Did what?" Maggie asked, then went right on as if the question and the answer were of no consequence. "There's more coffee cake if you want it. It's in the oven to keep it warm. And I just brewed a fresh pot of coffee. Help yourself. If we'd known you were coming, we'd have waited."

Jo tried to tamp down her irritation and act just as cool. She took off her coat, tossed it over a chair, retrieved the coffee cake, then poured herself some coffee before sitting down at the table. She cut herself a huge slice of the coffee cake as she inquired, "Who called Pete Catlett and sent him to my doorstep last night?"

Three perfectly bland expressions greeted her.

"Then he did come by?" Ashley said, confirming her role in getting him there. "Good."

"You seem upset," Melanie noted, looking more curious than repentant.

"I'm not upset," she said, struggling to keep her tone neutral. She thought she was doing an admirable job of it. "Just surprised."

"Everyone, including Ashley, says Pete does the best work of anyone in the area. Do you have a problem with letting him fix the porch?" Maggie asked.

"Yes, I have a problem with it," she blurted without thinking. Damn, damn, damn. So much for neutrality. She should have taken some other approach. Now she'd all but admitted that it was personal.

"Which is?" Maggie persisted.

Jo tried to backtrack and come up with an explanation that wouldn't stir up more questions. "You didn't consult me," she said finally. "It's got nothing to do with Pete. I'm sure he's very qualified, but I'm the one who's going to have to deal with having him underfoot day in and day out. He's there right now, brandishing some sort of weapon that smashes boards. I'll be lucky if the place is standing when I get back."

"Come on, Jo. Don't exaggerate. He knows what he's doing," Ashley soothed, then grinned. "And he's easy on the eye, don't you think? He did a lot of the work for us, when Josh and I were fixing up our place. If I'd been single, I'd have definitely given him a second look."

Jo rolled her eyes. She was beginning to get a much clearer picture. Pete's presence was a gift from her big sister, a male distraction, eye candy. Geez-oh-flip, she was distraught over a broken engagement and Ashley was serving up more testosterone. If only she and the others understood the irony of this particular gesture.

Jo glanced up and realized Melanie was studying her with obviously increased curiosity.

"Is there some particular reason you don't want Pete underfoot? I mean Pete specifically," Melanie inquired. "I wasn't even aware that you knew him, yet you seem to have taken an almost instant dislike to the man."

Jo sighed. That was not a road she intended to travel down, even with her sisters. Her life was pathetic enough in their eyes at the moment without rehashing ancient history. She'd already stirred up more suspicion than she'd intended to.

"I don't dislike him," she lied. "I just wish you'd let me find my own contractor. I have a broken heart, not a broken brain. I need to find things to do, if I'm going to stay here for a while. I can't just mope around the house all day. And despite what you think, looking at some hunk you've found for me is not the answer."

"It's an interesting start, though, don't you agree?" Ashley asked. "I'd think you'd be more appreciative."

Jo tried to muster up the expected gratitude, but all she could think of was just how badly their good intentions had gone awry.

"Have you spoken to him?" she asked Ashley instead. "Has he told you how long this job will take or how much it will cost? The man builds huge houses. I've seen the signs for them everywhere. He's bound to charge a fortune for a minor little repair like this. I'm sure someone else, a handyman for instance, could do the work for a lot less."

"Too late now, if Pete's already started. Besides, I told you not to worry about the cost," her big sister said. "And I trust Pete to do what needs to be done and to give me a reasonable price."

"Really?" she said skeptically. "You trust him?"

Ashley's antennae went on full alert. "Is there some reason you think I shouldn't? I thought you said you didn't know him."

Jo saw that she wasn't going to maneuver her sister into firing Pete, not without giving her something specific to go on. Since she wasn't about to admit the one thing that might have done it, she merely shrugged.

"It's your money," she told Ashley. "I suppose I can put up with him for however long this takes. I don't know how much thinking I'll get done with all that clatter going on, though."

"Just as well," Melanie said. "You're probably thinking too much. Forget about what happened in Boston. Forget about everything and relax."

Jo bit back a laugh. As if she could relax when she was brushing up against the past every time she turned around! "Sure. I'll try."

"Maybe I should stop by and tell Pete he needs to clear everything with you," Ashley suggested, her expression thoughtful. "That way you can decide when it's most convenient for him to be there. He's an accommodating guy."

"No," Jo said hurriedly. The last thing she wanted was to have her very perceptive big sister watching the interaction between her and Pete. "I'm sure we can devise some sort of schedule that works for both of us. I have no idea why I'm making such a big thing out of this. It's silly, really."

"Are you sure? The last thing I want to do is add more stress to your life," Ashley told her.

Too late for that, Jo thought. She plastered a smile on her face. "Not to worry," she assured Ashley. "I'm sorry I got you all worked up over this. It's not a big deal. Really." She stood up. "Now I've got to run."

"Run where?" Maggie asked. "You haven't even touched your coffee cake."

Somewhere, anywhere, Jo thought desperately. She grabbed up the slab of cake and wrapped it in a napkin. "Errands," she said succinctly. "I'll take this with me."

"I'll come with you," Melanie offered, pushing back her chair and standing. "I have some errands of my own."

Jo frowned at her. "I don't need a babysitter."

Melanie immediately sat back down. "Sorry."

Relenting, Jo crossed the room and gave her a hug. "I need to do things for myself, okay? It's not that I don't appreciate the offer."

"I know," Melanie said, regarding her with sympathetic understanding. "We're hovering."

"You're hovering," Jo confirmed.

"Okay, then, go off on your own, baby sister," Ashley said. "If you need us, all you have to do is call."

Jo grinned. "I have all your numbers on speed dial on my cell phone."

She hurried away before they remembered that down here in the boonies, her cell phone was virtually useless.

Pleased with herself, she noted that it was her second fast escape of the morning. At this rate, she was going to wind up being the family expert at quick getaways. Of course, unless she turned to bank robbery, it probably was a wasted talent.

Chapter Three

As he worked, Pete thought about how skittish Jo was around him. He couldn't honestly blame her, but it was more distressing than he cared to admit. Once they'd been as close as any two people could be. They'd sat out in the backyard swing right here at Rose Cottage with the moon overhead and the Chesapeake Bay lapping at the shore, and talked for hours on end. A fierce attraction had burned between them, but more than that, they'd been comfortable together, in tune with each other. They'd shared their hopes and dreams.

Jo had been the first person he'd told about his desire to build homes right here in Virginia's Northern Neck region. His uncle—his mother's brother—had taught him the construction trade, taught him all about being a craftsman who took pride in his materials and his work.

For as long as he could remember, Pete had wanted to follow in his Uncle Jeb's footsteps. Maybe that was only because Jeb was the only male role model in his life, but he didn't think so. If he'd had to explain it, he would have said it was because his uncle had shared with Pete his lifelong passion for crafting something strong and solid.

"I think it's because you want to build homes that will endure," Jo had said to him one night, picking up on an emotion Pete hadn't been able to express. "To make up for not having had one yourself. I'll bet you can see families living in the homes you build. I imagine you can hear the laughter and feel the love that you think you missed."

She'd understood him so well. Even at eighteen, she'd been able to put things into words that at twenty he'd barely recognized in himself—the hurts, the heartaches, the longings.

"We'll have a home like that," he'd promised her one night. "It will withstand the salt air, the winds, the storms. We'll fill it with kids and laughter. The only thing more solid will be our marriage."

Her eyes had been luminous in the moonlight. "I want that, Pete. More than you can imagine. Let's not wait too long."

"Just till you finish college and I'm established," he'd said, thinking they had all the time in the world.

She'd gone back to Boston a few days later to begin her freshman year at Boston University, and he'd buried himself in work. His uncle was a demanding taskmaster, but the long, hard days had been worth every backbreaking minute because he had a goal, making a life for himself that he would one day share with Jo. He'd been so sure that the first house he built entirely with his own hands would be for the two of them.

But then Kelsey, whom he'd known most of his life, had started hanging around. She'd never gone to college, either, but unlike Pete, she was in a dead-end job she hated at the local grocery store. Whenever she had the time, she was looking for uncomplicated, undemanding fun.

Pete saw no harm in going out with her for a few beers. They both knew the score. She even knew he was in love with Jo and claimed not to care. "I'll just keep your bed warm for her," she promised when they'd tumbled into it. He'd had too many beers to think with anything other than his hormones. It was stupid. It was irresponsible and reckless. He regretted it even before he realized that he hadn't used a condom. Then he'd known it was the worst mistake he'd ever made.

He hadn't been surprised when Kelsey had told him she was pregnant. He'd been waiting with dread for just that news. It meant the end of his relationship with Jo, the end of his dreams.

But he'd accepted responsibility with no argument. He'd offered marriage and was determined to make the best of it. There had even been a few months at the beginning when he'd thought it might work, mostly because he and Kelsey were so in love with the baby they'd created.

Then there had been the endless months when he'd been forced to accept that it wasn't working at all, would never work.

Even now, two years later, thinking about the misery of that time, about his son's tears when Kelsey had dragged Davey off to Richmond and away from his dad tore Pete apart. Distracted by his dark thoughts, he carelessly smashed his thumb with a hammer, then cursed.

"You'll ruin your reputation if people catch you doing stuff like that on the job," Josh Madison commented, startling Pete so badly that he almost whacked his thumb again.

Grateful to have an excuse for a break, Pete stepped away from the remains of the porch. "What brings you by?"

"Ashley mentioned you were going to do some work over here. Thought I'd stop by and say hi, see how things are going."

Pete's gaze narrowed at the hint that Josh was somehow here to supervise. Did they not entirely trust him, after all? "That deck I built for you guys okay?" he asked Josh.

Josh chuckled. "Couldn't be better. I'm not here to hassle you. I'm just killing time."

"Good to know." He gave Josh a curious look. "Things slow at your law practice?"

"Just right, actually. I have a lot of time for Ashley and for fishing. For the first time in my life, everything's in perfect balance."

"Sounds like every man's dream," Pete said enviously. Since he suspected there was something more on Josh's mind, he waited to see if Josh would get around to it without prodding.

"You getting along okay with Jo?" Josh asked eventually.

So that was it. Pete gave him a sharp look. "Why wouldn't I be?"

"Just wondering," Josh said innocently. "She's a little uptight these days. Just thought I'd warn you."

Pete nodded. "I'd noticed."

"Cut her some slack, okay? Ashley and the others are worried about her."

Pete was glad to hear that they shared his concern. He also realized this was his chance to dig a little deeper into the circumstances that had brought Jo to town. "Any idea what the problem is?"

"Broken engagement," Josh said. "Turns out the guy was a real jerk. She caught him cheating on her."

Pete's stomach fell. No wonder Jo was looking at him with even deeper disdain and distrust than he'd anticipated. She'd been twice burned by betrayal. He'd been the first, and now he was right here rubbing her nose in it when she was trying to recover from this latest heartbreak. His presence was probably going a long way toward reinforcing her impression that all men were worthless bastards.

"That's tough," he said, trying to keep any trace of emotion from his voice.

"I met the guy once," Josh said. "She brought him to the wedding when Ashley and I got married. To tell you the truth, I think she's better off, but that's not something she wants to hear right now, I'm sure."

Curiosity got the best of Pete. He wanted to know about the man Jo had chosen to marry, even if just thinking about her with someone else twisted his gut into knots. "You didn't like the guy?"

Josh shook his head.

"Any particular reason?"

"Let's just say he spent the wedding chatting up

every other woman in the room. Since most of them were members of Jo's family and married themselves, it seemed to me the handwriting was on the wall. He even put a couple of less-than-subtle moves on my wife. If I hadn't walked up when I did, I think Ashley would have decked him."

"Why the hell didn't she warn her sister?"

"I think she tried, but Jo didn't want to hear it. She was convinced Ashley had misread the man's intentions. She was sure he was just being friendly, hoping to get the family to warm up to him. The D'Angelos are a tightknit clan."

Pete regarded him intently. "Any chance Jo was right, that it was innocent?"

Josh laughed. "You know my wife. Does she strike you as someone who'd misread that kind of situation? No, she got it exactly right, and remember, I heard most of it, too." He shrugged. "But you know how people are when they're in love. They have to figure out their mistakes for themselves. And there's not a more loyal, trusting woman around than Jo. She didn't want to believe the worst."

"I suppose," Pete said, his guilt stirring all over again. Jo had trusted him once, and look what he'd done. She was probably convinced now that her judgment about men sucked. That meant it was going to be a whole lot harder for him to convince her otherwise.

Josh regarded him curiously. "You seem awfully interested."

"You know me. I'm a sucker for a woman in distress."

"I doubt she'd want your pity."

Pete laughed. "No kidding. I do have a few functioning brain cells. There hasn't been a woman born who wants a man coming around out of pity." He studied Josh curiously. "Why'd you tell me all this? Just so I'd keep an eye out for her?"

Josh rolled his eyes. "Come on, Catlett, get serious. Everyone in town knows your reputation. Since your divorce, you date a lot, but you don't get serious. Let's just consider this conversation fair warning. Jo's vulnerable. A lot of people will be upset if you hurt her."

Little did he know, Pete thought wryly.

"Yeah, I'll keep that in mind," Pete promised. "I'll try not to jump her bones first chance I get."

Josh scowled at him, clearly taking the comment at face value. "I'm trusting you to keep that promise."

He was gone before Pete could reply. Of course, the truth was that he hadn't needed Josh's warning to know to take things slowly with Jo. She had warning signs posted around her that all but shouted her vulnerability.

And even if she hadn't, she'd made it abundantly clear that she was strictly off-limits to Pete in particular.

Of course, he admitted to himself, that only made things interesting. There was nothing on earth that Pete liked better than a challenge. That it happened to be provided by a woman he'd once loved just made it that much more fascinating.

Jo managed to hide out till dusk, certain that once the light died Pete would be forced to quit for the day.

Now she stood in the front yard and gaped at what had once been the porch. It was a yawning, empty space that stretched out between where she was and the door. Four-by-four posts propped up the porch roof.

Thanks to the dimming light and shadows, getting inside suddenly seemed treacherous. The only alternative was to go around back, but she wasn't even sure if her key worked in that lock, which raised something of a quandary. How the devil was she supposed to get inside without crawling over the threshold in some awkward spectacle?

She was still pondering her choices when the front door opened, startling her so badly, she dropped the bags she was carrying. Thankfully, nothing she'd bought on her shopping spree was breakable.

"There you are," Pete called out from inside. "I was wondering when you'd be back. I didn't want to leave till you turned up."

Jo frowned. His presence was precisely why she'd stayed away so long. She'd hoped to outwait him. She should have guessed he'd stay put just to be perverse.

"Where's your truck? Did you deliberately hide it?"

He grinned. "Took it home and walked back," he admitted. "I figured you'd turn right around and leave if you saw it parked out here."

"Damn straight," she muttered.

His grin broadened. "Still stubborn as a mule, I see. Come on, Jo. What's the big deal? I thought you might have some trouble getting inside, so I stuck around. End of story. I didn't stay just to annoy you."

He glanced at the bags now scattered at her feet. "Did you buy out the stores?"

"Only a few of them," she said, regarding him warily. "Since you're here, make yourself useful and open the back door."

"Why haul all that stuff around back when you can come in this way?"

"How do you suggest I step up and into the house?"

"You always have me to help," he suggested. "That's why I'm here, after all."

Jo couldn't see his eyes at this distance and in this light, but she suspected there was a wicked glint in them. "You?" she asked skeptically.

He leaped down, then came toward her. When he was closer, she could spot the amusement glittering in his eyes. She backed up a step, bent over and grabbed haphazardly for the bags, holding them in front of her as if they would somehow ward him off.

He just kept coming. "Hope none of that stuff you're carrying weighs too much," he joked as he scooped her up, then shifted her till she was snuggled securely against his chest. "Nope. Light as a feather."

"Pete, put me down this instant," Jo grumbled, even though the faint scent of his aftershave and the masculine scent that was as familiar to her as salt air made her feel vaguely weak with a sudden, unwanted longing.

He stopped in his tracks and gazed into her eyes. "Now, the way I see it, you have two choices. You can let me give you a little boost inside or you can face the indignity of trying to scramble up there on your own while I stand here and watch." He grinned. "I imagine it'll be quite a show. You always did have the cutest little butt around."

"You're a pig!"

"You're not the first to suggest that," he noted calmly. "So, what's it going to be?"

"Just get me into the damn house and then go away," she said.

"You'd send me away even after I got dinner all ready for the two of us?"

"I would send you away if you'd spent your last dime on it," she said firmly.

"Heartless," he said mildly. "I'd never have guessed it."

"Some traits develop over time," she commented wryly as he stepped onto a precarious arrangement of cinder blocks she hadn't even noticed, then stepped inside the house as easily as if there were actual steps.

"Why didn't you just tell me you'd rigged up some temporary steps? I could have gotten in here on my own," she noted, punching him in the chest.

"True," he agreed, his grin unrepentant. "But this was more fun."

"Not for me," she said, scrambling out of his arms and snatching away her packages. "Go away."

"Not till you eat."

"I told you you weren't invited to stay for dinner," she said, even as she sniffed the air and noticed the appealing aroma of baking chicken.

"That's fine, but I don't intend to leave until I see you put a few forkfuls of food into your mouth."

"Do I look as if I need coaxing to eat?"

"Yes," he said readily. "You're too skinny. It was the first thing I noticed when I saw you last night."

"Now you're just being insulting."

"That's me, known far and wide for my complete lack of charm. Dinner's in five minutes, if you want to put this stuff away and wash up."

Jo sighed and accepted the fact that she wasn't getting rid of him. She didn't pretend to understand why he was insinuating himself into her life like this. Maybe Ashley had hired him to do more than fix the porch and look good while he was at it. Maybe he was an undercover babysitter. Whatever was keeping him around, he seemed to be serious about it. She knew from bitter experience that he wouldn't be shaken off till he was good and ready. That's why it had hurt so much when he'd simply vanished without a word seven years ago. It had told her he was ready, if not eager, to be rid of her and move on to his new life.

"If you're staying, you may as well eat," she finally said grudgingly.

"Thank you," he said solemnly.

To her surprise, the table was set. He'd even lit a couple of candles and plunked a bouquet of flowers in a water glass in the center of the table. It had all the trappings of romance to it, and a tiny little shiver of anticipation danced along her spine.

"What's all this?" she asked suspiciously, as if it weren't plain as day.

"Ambience," he said, looking vaguely uncomfortable. "I hear women are fond of it."

"Maybe when they're being courted, but the circumstances are a bit different with us."

"Are they?" he asked in a tone clearly intended to have her blood humming.

She regarded him with frustration. "Pete, you can't say stuff like that."

"Why not?"

"It's not appropriate."

"Because we parted a long time ago?"

"No, idiot. Because you're married and have at least one child. What is wrong with you? You can't start hitting on me. I am not going to have a fling with a married man just for old time's sake."

Something dark and painful flashed in his eyes. "Thanks for the vote of confidence about my morals," he said tightly. "Just to set the record straight, I have a son who lives in Richmond with his mother. I'm no longer married."

Jo had picked up a glass of water, but her hand shook so badly she had to set it down again. His news was the last thing she'd expected. It changed everything. It made her nervous in ways she hadn't been before. His marriage had been like a safety net, the only thing keeping her from forgetting about all the anguish he'd caused her.

"You're divorced, not separated?" she asked, just to be sure she'd gotten it right.

"Two years now. I can bring the divorce papers by for you, if you don't believe me," he said, his expression bleak.

"What happened?" she asked instinctively.

He gave her a shuttered look. "I don't want to talk about it."

"But—"

Now he was the one on the defensive. "Look, I fixed you a little dinner and stuck around to make sure you ate it. No big deal. It doesn't give you the right to start poking around in my personal life."

"You tried to poke around in mine," she reminded him.

"And you told me to butt out. Now I see your point. Let's stick to safe, neutral topics."

Jo nodded, but somewhere deep inside, where Pete's announcement had lit a ridiculous spark of hope, she realized that things would never be entirely safe or neutral between her and this man.

She swallowed a whole litany of questions and searched frantically for something they could talk about.

"The chicken looks good," she said eventually. "When did you learn to cook?"

"After the divorce," he said, his gaze avoiding hers.

So, not even dinner was a safe topic, apparently. Jo regarded him with frustration. "You could help me out here. Say something."

An unwilling smile tugged at the corners of his mouth. It was obvious he was fighting it. "There never was much that was safe or simple between us, was there?"

"Not much," she admitted.

"There's always the weather," he said. "I hear it might snow again."

She went along with him. "Really? When?"

He did grin then. "Sometime this winter."

Jo laughed and the tension was broken. "You made that up, didn't you?"

"Hey, it's as accurate a forecast as any we're likely to get on the news," he protested.

"I suppose so." She grinned back at him. "Think it will rain this spring?"

"Pretty certain," he said.

"If we work at this, we could carve out whole new careers for ourselves."

"Personally I like the one I have," Pete said. "You can go for it if you want to."

She shook her head. "Not me. I like landscape design."

Pete's eyes lit up. "That's what you do?"

"Yes," she said, surprised by his apparent enthusiasm. "Why?"

"I don't suppose you're looking for any work while you're here, are you?"

"Mike said he might have some jobs for me," she admitted. "We haven't discussed the specifics, though."

He nodded slowly. "You could work through him," he said. "Or work directly for me. I've been on his waiting list for weeks for a couple of houses I just built. He told me the other day he might have help soon. I imagine that's you."

Jo swallowed hard. So there really was more work around than Mike could handle, but working for Pete? Could she do it? Wasn't that just asking for disaster? She needed more information on just how closely she'd have to work with him. It might be smarter to keep Mike as a buffer.

"Are you making the decisions?" she asked. "Or are the new owners of the houses?"

"I'm making the decisions for now. I've built these places on spec. I want the grounds in good shape by spring when the real estate market kicks into high gear around here." He studied her intently. "Is that a problem?"

She put her fork down and met his gaze. "I don't know. Is it, Pete?"

"What are you asking me?"

"It's been a long time. I was a girl when you knew me. Now, not only am I a woman, but I'm a professional. Can you treat me with the respect I deserve and trust my judgment? Or will our personal history constantly be getting in the way?"

"I could ask you the same thing," he reminded her.

Her lips curved. "But I asked first."

His gaze never wavered. "I always trusted you. I'm the one who blew it, Jo, not you. I may not have shown you the respect you deserved at the end, but the whole mess was caused by my stupidity. It had nothing to do with the way I felt about you. I know that doesn't make a lot of sense, since you were the one who got hurt."

"No, it doesn't," she said.

"I guess the real question is whether you trust me enough to give me another chance, at least enough for us to work together on a few projects. We can take it one day at a time. Anytime you say it's not working for you, that's it. No hard feelings."

"I don't walk out on jobs," she said. "I'll finish whatever I start. You can count on that."

"And you can count on me not to hurt you again, Jo. I mean that."

Sincerity radiated from him. Jo wanted desperately to believe what he was saying. He clearly was talking about a whole lot more than a couple of landscaping jobs, but the work was all she could think about for now. It was a start, and it would keep her from going stir-crazy here.

She finally held out her hand. "Deal. I'm going to want to clear this with Mike, but if he doesn't have a problem with it, I'll do it."

"Sounds fair to me." Pete took her hand in his, but instead of shaking it, he raised it to his lips and kissed her knuckles. "You won't regret it, darlin'."

She kept her gaze on his steady and cautious. "I hope you're right," she said softly. For both their sakes.

Chapter Four

First thing the next morning, Jo opened the back door to Mike and, to her dismay, Melanie. She frowned at her sister.

"I didn't know you were coming," she said.

"Mike said you'd asked him to stop by, so I figured I'd tag along." Melanie returned her gaze curiously. "Is that a problem?"

Jo bit back a sigh. She'd really hoped to have this conversation with Mike in private. She was afraid her sister would read too much into it. Too late for that now. She could hardly kick her out. Melanie really would read too much into that.

Jo forced a smile. "Of course not," she said with exaggerated cheer that was as phony as her smile. Hopefully it was too early in the day for Melanie to pick up on that. "Come on in. The coffee's ready. Have you two eaten? I can scramble some eggs, or make you some toast at least. I'm afraid if you want baked goods, you're at the wrong place. That's Maggie's province."

"I'll pass," Melanie said, still regarding her with a puzzled look.

"Me, too," Mike replied. "I have to be on a job site in twenty minutes. I'd have been here sooner, but I had to wait for my wife to get ready. It's actually astounding how fast she can move when she's highly motivated."

"Oh?" Jo asked.

"She was dying of curiosity about why you wanted to see me," Mike said, giving his wife an affectionate look.

"Then I'll get right to the reason I called," Jo told him. "Pete Catlett has asked if I'd be willing to do the landscape design for a couple of houses he built. He said you were too busy to get to them right away. I said I'd do it, but only if you didn't have a problem with it. I don't want to poach on one of your clients."

"Hell, no, I don't have a problem with it." Mike grinned. "That would be great, in fact. Pete's been very patient. The minute Melanie told me you were coming, I started hoping you'd agree to take on those jobs, but I didn't want to rush you."

Although he sounded very convincing, Jo pressed him. "You're sure? We can work it out so you bill him and then you can pay me whatever you figure the going rate is around here."

"Absolutely not," Mike said. "Why make extra paperwork? Make your deal directly with Pete. I don't need to be involved." He gave her a sly look. "Although, if you decide you want to work around here on a more permanent basis, I'd like you to consider teaming up with me. There's more than enough work for a partnership."

Melanie's eyes lit up. "What a fabulous idea!"

Jo frowned at her. "As if you weren't the one who planted it in his head."

"I most certainly did not," Melanie retorted. "This was Mike's idea."

Jo glanced at him. He nodded in confirmation.

"In that case, thanks. I appreciate the offer. I'll think about it. Let's see how these two jobs go first. You might hate my ideas."

"Don't wait. Say yes now, Jo," her sister pleaded. "It would be so great to have you living here."

"She's right," Mike agreed. "It would sure help me out."

Jo held up her hands. "Hey, slow down, you two. I've agreed to take on a couple of jobs. Even if I agreed to do a few more, I'm not making some long-term commitment. I still intend to go back to Boston at some point."

"But why?" Melanie asked. "This is perfect for you. You'd be your own boss, instead of working for someone who doesn't really appreciate you. And who knows? If you settled here, maybe Mom and Dad would retire down here. Wouldn't that be fantastic?"

Things were moving way too quickly for Jo. "Don't get ahead of yourself. Mom and Dad are nowhere near ready to retire and, despite what you think of my boss, I did tell him I'd be back. It was very generous of him to give me a leave of absence."

"An *unpaid* leave," Melanie retorted. "Where's the generosity in that?"

"He could have hired someone else for that position," Jo argued.

"In winter?" Melanie asked skeptically, then gave a gesture of surrender. "Okay, okay, I won't push."

Jo hooted at that. None of her sisters were the shy, retiring type. They'd push like crazy, especially if they sensed she was weakening. "Yeah, right."

"I promise," Melanie said, sketching a little *X* across her heart. "The decision's all yours, even if your staying would mean that Mike and I would have more time to work on our baby project."

Jo stared at her sister. "Baby project?"

"We think it's time Jessie had a little sister or brother," Melanie said. "But Mike's so busy, we barely even see each other, much less have time to, well, you know."

Mike nudged her in the ribs. "We will always find time for that, sweetheart." He winked at Jo. "On that note, I think I'll get out of here. I meant what I said, Jo. The door's always open if you do decide to stay, even if it's just through spring. That's my busiest season and it's worse than ever with all the construction going on."

She stood up and impulsively gave him a hug. "You're the best."

"So my wife tells me," he said lightly, dropping a kiss on Melanie's lips before taking off.

As soon as the door was closed behind him, Melanie regarded her intently. "Now we can get to the good stuff."

Jo stared at her blankly. "What good stuff?"

"You and Pete. You seem to have formed a bond awfully quickly."

Jo frowned. This was exactly what she'd been afraid

would happen the minute any of her sisters heard about this job. "It's not a bond. I mentioned that I do landscape design. He said he needed help. That's it."

Melanie obviously wasn't satisfied. "And when did you share this information?"

Jo saw the trap. "Yesterday," she said cautiously.

"Oh? I thought you intended to stay away as long as he was working."

"That was the plan," Jo agreed. "It didn't work out. Turned out he was still here when I got home."

"What time was that?"

"Melanie, is there some point you're trying to make?"

"No," she said cheerfully. "I'm just fishing for information I can share with Maggie and Ashley. It's so rare that I know anything before they do."

"And what is it you think you know?"

"That something's clicking between you and Pete."

"Indeed there is," Jo said. "He's thrilled about my job experience. I'm excited about his offer to pay me for my expertise. If that's clicking, then we are definitely on the same wavelength."

"Joke if you want, but I think there's more going on," Melanie insisted.

"Such as?"

"Chemistry."

"More like botany," Jo said dryly. "We have plants in common."

"Ha-ha," Melanie responded with a roll of her eyes.

"I thought it was amusing."

"Where is he, by the way?"

"Working, I imagine."

"But not here?" Melanie said, looking disappointed

that she wasn't going to get to put him through the wringer on this visit.

"Not till later," Jo said.

Melanie brightened at once. "After hours? How much work can he actually get done once it's dark?"

Jo groaned at her sister's determination to make something of the situation. She would have expected it from Ashley or Maggie, but Melanie usually had better sense. "I think maybe this whole baby project of yours has put your mind on a single track," she told her.

Melanie beamed. "Could be. Mike and I certainly don't think about much else." She gave Jo a pointed look. "At least when we get five minutes alone together."

"Oh, no, you don't, big sister," Jo chided. "You are not going to guilt me into staying here, just so you and your husband can have more sex."

"It's not about the sex. It's about a baby," Melanie said. "A little niece or nephew for you. Wouldn't that be wonderful?"

"Wonderful," Jo agreed readily. "But making it happen isn't my responsibility."

Melanie laughed. "Oh, well, it was worth a shot. Now I have to be going. I have things to do and places to go."

"I imagine Maggie's will be your first stop," Jo said.

Her sister didn't even try to pretend otherwise. "Of course," she said at once. "Want to come?"

Something told Jo it was the only way to protect her own interests. Otherwise Maggie and Ashley would only hear Melanie's spin on the news that she was going to do a little work for Pete. That would only fuel their eagerness to turn it into a budding romance. And once

inspired, who knew what lengths they'd go to in order
to make sure that love bloomed by spring, right along
with the forsythia?

She gave Melanie a cheerful smile. "I'll be right behind you."

She knew she'd made the right decision when Melanie didn't even try to hide her disappointment.

When Pete finally caught up with him, Mike had a
sketchbook in hand and was apparently trying to rough
in a landscape design for a piece of waterfront property
on which a Cape Cod-style house was under construction. Unfortunately, it was so damn cold out that he was
forced to wear gloves and he kept dropping his pencil.

Pete retrieved it from the ground and handed it to
him. "Ever think of doing this inside your truck with the
motor running and the heater blasting? The wind off the
bay cuts right through you this morning."

Mike gave him a sour look. "I noticed. Unfortunately,
the builder piled all his construction debris beside the
house. There's no way around it except on foot. That
means I get to stand out here and freeze my butt off and
hope my hand's not shaking so badly that I won't recognize what I've sketched in."

"If you were working with me, you wouldn't have
that problem," Pete told him.

Mike gave him a hard look. "But I hear you've found
yourself a backup landscape designer."

Pete regarded him with surprise. "You know?"

"Jo called last night. I stopped by to see her on my
way over here. She told me. She wanted to be sure I had
no objections."

"Do you?"

"Not a one. She'll do a good job for you. I've seen some of the places she landscaped up in Boston. She's good at it."

"Boston's not here. You sure she'll understand what plants work in this climate?"

"Hold it," Mike said. "Let's have this conversation in your truck. Something tells me it's going to require my full attention. Your heater will probably warm up faster than mine, since you just got here."

"And there's coffee," Pete said. "I picked up an extra cup in case you were in this precise predicament. Some builders aren't nearly as thoughtful as I am." He winked. "Just one reason you ought to make my jobs your first priority."

When they were finally settled in the cab of Pete's truck with the heater blasting, Mike gave him a hard look. "Okay, what's up? What's with the crack about me making you my first priority? I thought you were content with having Jo do the work. Are you having second thoughts about that?"

Pete weighed his response. He didn't want to get into all the complicated reasons why it might be a bad idea. Those had only started churning in his head after he'd left Rose Cottage the night before. By morning, he'd concluded he ought to try to find some way out of their agreement. Her qualifications were the only legitimate excuse he could come up with.

"You have to admit this area requires a different approach than some house in suburban Boston," he said defensively.

"Her credentials are impeccable," Mike said. "She'll

do her homework, Pete. You don't need to worry about that. And she'll show you site plans and sketches, same as I would. You have any questions, you can bring 'em to me."

Pete knew how that would go over if Jo found out he was taking her work to Mike behind her back. "You know I can't do that. It's insulting."

Mike grinned. "Glad you have sense enough to see that. Now tell me what's really going on here. It's not about Jo's experience, is it?"

Pete tried a different tack. "She's got a lot going on in her life right now. Josh told me about the broken engagement and I've seen for myself that she's an emotional wreck. Maybe she shouldn't be taking on work."

Mike studied him intently, then began to chuckle. "You're scared of her, aren't you?"

Pete glowered at him. "Why on earth would I be scared of a little bitty thing like Jo D'Angelo?"

"Maybe because you're attracted to her," Mike suggested. His expression sobered. "I know about the two of you, pal. I know you had a thing once."

Pete slapped his hand on the steering wheel in frustration. "Dammit, where'd you hear about that?" he demanded, knowing even as he asked that he was giving himself away. "I know you weren't around back then."

"Then it's true?"

Pete nodded. "What exactly did you hear?"

"That the two of you had a summer fling, maybe more than that."

"It was more than that," Pete admitted. "And I broke her heart. Do her sisters know about that?"

"I don't think so," Mike said. "You'd never have set

foot inside Rose Cottage if they knew. In fact, Ashley would most likely have taken a shotgun to you when you showed up to do that work for her and Josh."

"That's what I figured." He gave Mike a worried look. "Are you going to tell them?"

"Not unless it seems like you're going to hurt her again. You and I are friends, Pete, but Jo's family now. I have to look out for her."

"I respect that," Pete said. "I certainly don't want to hurt her again, but I'm wondering if we should start spending quite so much time together when there's all this past history that needs to be resolved."

Mike's expression turned thoughtful. "Okay now, it's a given that I'm no expert on women, not even my wife, but it seems to me if Jo agreed to do this, then she's ready to spend more time with you. Maybe this is your chance to make things right with her. A couple of jobs will give you plenty of uncomplicated time together."

"It gets complicated when we're in the same room," Pete said dryly.

Mike laughed. "A whole lot of pheromones bouncing around?"

"You have no idea."

"Okay, this is definitely a guy approach, but maybe you should just take her to bed and get all that out of the way," Mike suggested.

Pete gave him a horrified look. "Her engagement just broke up. She's an emotional mess. And you want me to take her to bed?"

"Just a thought," Mike said.

Pete shook his head. "How the hell did you ever land a classy woman like Melanie?"

"I didn't. She landed me."

"I hope you count your blessings every night," Pete told him.

"Believe me, I do. Every night and every morning," Mike said fervently. "So, are you okay with this work arrangement? You're going to let Jo do the design work?"

"Yes," Pete said. And he'd suffer the torment of the damned every single minute he was around her.

It was nearly dark when Pete finally pulled up at Rose Cottage with a load of lumber. Jo heard the truck rumble into the yard, grabbed a jacket and went outside and around to the front of the house to meet him.

"I was expecting you earlier," she said as he jumped down from the cab of the truck.

"Sorry. I got held up. I ran into problems on every job this morning."

"Anything major?"

He shook his head. "Nope. Just time-consuming. I figured I'd drop this lumber off tonight, then come by first thing in the morning to get in an hour or two of work here before I head over to the house I'm building in White Stone. I thought maybe you'd like to go with me, since that's one of the ones I'd like you to landscape."

"Sure." She studied him curiously. He hadn't once looked directly at her. "Pete, is everything okay? You seem a little distracted."

"Just one of those days, I guess." He began pulling the boards off the back of his truck and stacking them neatly.

Without being asked, Jo went to help him, but as she reached for a board, he scowled at her. "What do you think you're doing?"

"Helping."

"You don't need to do that."

"But I can, so why shouldn't I?" she asked, meeting his gaze. There was something dark and dangerous in his eyes, a look she couldn't quite interpret.

"I'm getting paid to do the job," he said, trying to nudge her aside.

"And I imagine you're being paid by the hour, so if I help, it will cost Ashley less," she said, grabbing for another board.

"Jo!"

She bit back a grin at the frustration in his voice. "Yes, Pete?"

His fierce look finally vanished and he sighed. "What am I supposed to do with you?"

"Let me help," she suggested lightly.

"I don't think that's the answer," he said, and took a step toward her.

"Pete?"

"Yes, Jo," he said, a smile tugging at his lips.

"What are you doing?"

"Give it a minute and I'm sure you'll figure it out," he said softly, just before he lowered his lips to hers.

She should have protested. She should have pushed him away. But his kisses had lived in her memory for so long, how could she resist a chance to see if she'd gotten it right?

His taste was as familiar to her as her morning coffee. The texture of his lips was soft. His tongue was wickedly clever. A tiny spark turned into a full-fledged conflagration in a matter of seconds, just as it always had.

It wasn't supposed to be like this. She was supposed

to be over him, not putty in his hands. She wanted to mold herself to his body, wanted his hands to work their inevitable magic, but he seemed to be satisfied with the kiss. In fact, he seemed dedicated to perfecting it.

Her head was spinning, her knees were weak and her body was on fire when he finally dragged his mouth away with obvious reluctance. *No, no, no,* she wanted to protest, but she couldn't summon up the strength to utter a word.

Calling herself every kind of idiot under the sun, Jo stepped away from him and grabbed onto the truck for support. At least, Pete looked a little dazed, she decided, taking some satisfaction in that. It would be hell knowing that he'd emerged from that kiss unscathed, while her whole world had been rocked.

"Why did you do that?" she asked shakily.

"Because I had to," he said. "I couldn't survive one more second without it."

Her lips quirked. "Really?"

He laughed. "Don't be smug, darlin'. It's not becoming."

"I thought maybe you kissed me because I was annoying you," she retorted.

"And if that had been the reason, would you be on your best behavior from here on out?"

Jo considered the question, then shook her head. "No. Actually I think I'd go right on annoying you."

"And damn the consequences?"

"Pretty much."

He gave her a curious look. "You've changed."

"We all do."

"But this goes deeper than changing hairstyles or getting a college education."

"Oh?"

"You're obviously willing to play with fire."

Jo thought about that with a sense of shock. Was she? Ten minutes ago she would have sworn that the opposite was true, that she never wanted to take another emotional risk in her life. That kiss had changed everything.

"Maybe I am," she said slowly, then regarded him with an innocent expression. "Is that a problem?"

Pete stared at her for a very long time before a grin spread across his face. "Not for me."

"Okay, then, let's get the rest of this lumber off the truck and after that I'll fix dinner." She met his gaze. "If you're free."

He hesitated then. "This is just about dinner, right?"

She wanted to throw caution completely to the wind and say no, that it was about seduction, but some lingering shred of common sense crept in. This was the man who'd almost destroyed her, after all.

"It's just about dinner," she confirmed.

Pete nodded. "Good to know."

Because he looked so sweet trying to hide his disappointment, she couldn't resist adding, "I'll let you know about dessert later."

That ought to keep his hormones twisted in a knot all through dinner, she thought with satisfaction. Maybe she had a wicked streak, after all.

If so, nobody deserved to see it in action more than this man, who'd left her questioning everything about herself seven years ago. Maybe they'd met again just so he could help her restore her self-esteem and move on with her life.

Chapter Five

Pete was pretty sure if Jo so much as brushed up against him, he was going to go up in flames. That kiss had reminded him of the way they were together, and he knew he wasn't going to shake the memory anytime soon. Hell, five years of marriage—some of it actually good—hadn't dimmed the memory of the way she'd once come apart in his arms.

Face it, he told himself, Jo was seared into his heart and his soul.

Worse, though, than the stirring of old memories was that deliberate little taunt she'd uttered about dessert. They both knew she wasn't talking about apple pie. Sweet heaven, the woman had turned into a temptress. He wasn't sure how he felt about that. He'd liked her just fine when she'd been a shy, inexperienced young girl. He had a feeling the woman might just turn out to be too much for him.

He thought of Mike's advice to take her to bed and get the whole sexual attraction thing out of the way, but he now knew better than ever that it wouldn't be like that. Once they slept together again, there would be no turning back, at least not for him.

That would be all well and good if they were on the same page, but how could they be? His life was chaotic. His son was his first priority, which shouldn't be half as complicated as Kelsey tended to make it. How could he drag Jo into that, especially when it was the very situation that had hurt her so deeply years ago? Add in Josh's warning that Pete not hurt her, and any involvement was bound to be risky business.

And her life was no less complicated. Some other man had broken her heart, quite recently if Pete understood what she and others had told him. Much as he might like to believe that the man meant nothing to her, he doubted that was true. If Jo had given her heart to him, then she hadn't walked away from his betrayal unscathed. The shadows in her eyes had been proof enough of that.

Thankfully, it appeared he wasn't going to have to resolve the whole dilemma tonight. By the time they were inside, Jo seemed to have lost that feisty edge that had scared him to death. Obviously she was beset by second thoughts, too. In fact, she was suddenly giving him such a wide berth, it was almost insulting, as if she feared he was the one who'd put moves on her she wasn't ready to handle.

After putting up with her undisguised skittishness for

several minutes, Pete knew they had to settle things between them. He stepped in front of her and grasped her shoulders. Alarm immediately flared in her eyes.

"What?" she asked, her voice shaky with obvious nerves.

"Listen to me, Jo," he said quietly. "Nothing is going to happen between us tonight." He was pleased by the faint flicker of disappointment that registered on her face, but he stuck to his guns. "I'm going to stay for dinner. Then I'm going to give you a chaste peck on the cheek and go home to my own bed."

The declaration put some color back into her cheeks. "Oh, really? What makes you think you get to decide that's how the evening is going to go?"

Pete laughed at the show of feistiness. "Did you have another ending in mind?"

As he'd expected, she faltered at that. "No," she finally admitted.

"Okay, then, let's just agree to the ground rules, so you can stop looking like a deer I've caught in my headlights."

"I just wanted to prove how sophisticated I've become," she grumbled, stepping past him and chopping an onion with a ferocity that gave him chills.

He finally worked up the courage to ask her what the devil she meant by that.

She gave him a helpless shrug. "I honestly don't know. I suppose so you wouldn't think I'm some basket case who'd jump into bed with you on the rebound."

He hid a smile at that. "So if you had jumped into bed with me tonight, that would have been the only reason—the rebound thing?"

She nodded.

"Oh, darlin', don't make me prove you wrong about that," he said seriously.

"You can't prove me wrong, because it's the truth," she declared, her eyes flashing with defiance.

Pete couldn't resist calling her on it. "I've got five bucks and a kiss that says otherwise," he said, slapping a bill on the counter.

Her eyes widened with shock. "Are you crazy?"

"More than likely."

She forced the money back into his pocket, then immediately stepped gingerly away as if she'd belatedly realized her mistake. "I am not going to kiss you and I'm certainly not going to make a bet that says you can't seduce me."

"Because you know I'm right," he said, satisfied with the admission.

She frowned at him, and for a minute it seemed as if she might continue the debate until Pete was forced to kiss her to prove his point. Unfortunately, though, she finally drew in a deep breath and leveled a cool look into his eyes. "Would you prefer green beans or peas with dinner?"

Pete knew better than to laugh at the quick retreat to neutral turf. She might have felt compelled to take him up on his impulsive bet and, truthfully, he wasn't the least bit sure if he would have been able to resist.

The kitchen was filled with the scent of onions and garlic and tomato as Jo's spaghetti sauce simmered on the stove, but it was the pheromones swirling in the air that were getting to Jo. Somehow in the last few hours, she'd completely lost her mind. What she'd been doing ever since Pete had arrived rivaled the stupidity of waving a red cape at a bull. Did she want the man to seduce her?

Okay, yes, of course, she did. At least she wanted to know that he wanted to take her to bed. And it *was* about the rebound thing, no matter what he said to the contrary. She wanted to prove to herself that she was still a desirable woman, and who better to prove that than a man who'd once walked away from her? If she could attract Pete now, wouldn't that prove…something?

She tried to figure out what exactly it would prove and couldn't. Maybe it would only prove that she really was an idiot.

"How about some wine with dinner?" Pete asked. "I found a bottle of merlot in the wine rack."

Not a chance in hell, Jo thought. She needed all her wits about her if she was going to negotiate the mine-field she'd set up for herself tonight.

"No, thanks, but you have some if you'd like."

He shrugged. "I'm okay with a beer. Are there any in the fridge?"

"There should be," she said, opening the door. There were half a dozen bottles of beer inside. She took one out, twisted off the top and handed it to him. "Want a glass?"

"Nope. The bottle will do." He kept his gaze locked with hers. "Anything I can do to help with dinner?"

"The sauce is almost ready. You can drain the pasta, if you want to."

He put his bottle on the table and picked up the heavy pot, held it over the colander and dumped in the boiling water and pasta. More of the angel hair slithered down the drain than into the colander.

Jo chuckled as he tried to grab a handful. "Let it go,"

she said. "I made more than enough. We won't starve if some of it gets away."

He gave her a frustrated look. "You didn't warn me how slippery it would be."

"Haven't you ever cooked pasta before?"

"Sure," he said. "From a can."

Jo rolled her eyes. "Please don't ever let Maggie hear you say that. You'll absolutely destroy her respect for you. She thinks it's disgusting enough that I don't own a pasta machine so I can make my own."

"If Davey wants spaghetti, we go out," Pete said defensively. "I like the stuff in the can."

"See if you can still say that after we've eaten tonight," Jo said. "Of course, Maggie is right about one thing. This would be even better if we'd made the noodles from scratch."

He regarded her with surprise. "You can do that?"

"If you're asking if it's possible for a person to make pasta in his own kitchen, the answer is yes. If you want to know if I personally can do it, then, no. I'm hopeless at anything complicated—piecrusts and pasta are beyond me. The prepared stuff suits me just fine."

He grinned. "Nice to know there are some principles you're willing to compromise."

"Not the important ones."

She watched as he expertly wound some of the angel hair onto his fork, then took his first bite of the homemade sauce that was one of her Italian father's specialties. He'd insisted all his daughters learn the recipe. "It's a family tradition," Max D'Angelo had told them. "I won't have it dying out with me, so no matter what else you learn to cook, you'll learn this sauce."

Maggie was the only one who'd inherited his love of cooking, but the rest of them at least had this one dish they could use to impress guests. Pete was no exception. He regarded her with an expression bordering on awe.

"I think I love you," he said after his first bite.

Jo's pulse jumped, but she ignored it. "That's the sauce talking," she assured him…and herself. "I'll send some home with you. You can freeze it and try it out on your son next time he visits."

"If you think I'm sharing this with a kid who eats peanut butter and mayo sandwiches, you're nuts. It would be wasted on him."

"I'm sharing it with a man who likes spaghetti from a can," she reminded him.

"Not anymore," he said fervently. "I'll be here once a week for spaghetti. I'm writing that clause into whatever terms we set up for working together."

They ate for a while in silence, but Jo finally worked up the courage to bring up the one topic they'd avoided from the moment Pete had turned up on her doorstep. She figured he'd opened the door by mentioning his son's love of spaghetti.

She swallowed hard, then asked hesitantly, "Tell me about your son."

Pete's eyes lit up at once. "He's something. Sometimes I look at him and marvel that I had anything to do with creating such a great kid."

She swallowed the envy crawling up the back of her throat. "Does he look like you?"

"He looks a lot like I did when I was his age, the same dark hair, dark eyes and the exact same stubborn chin."

Jo smiled, thinking about the handful of pictures she'd once seen of Pete as a kid. He'd had a snaggle-toothed smile and a dimple that wouldn't quit. She hoped there was no trace of the sadness she was feeling in her eyes when she asked, "Do you have a picture of him?"

"Sure." He pulled his wallet out of his pocket and flipped it open, then handed it to her. "That's his school picture. He's in first grade. Believe me, he's not normally that neat. I'm sure five seconds after they took it, his shirt was tugged out of his pants and probably torn. He reminds me of that kid in the *Peanuts* comic strip, the one who's always going around in a cloud of dust. That's Davey. Five minutes out of the tub and he looks like he's gone ten rounds in the mud."

"He sounds wonderful," Jo said wistfully.

So many times over the past seven years she'd wondered about Pete's child. A part of her had respected his refusal to turn his back on the boy's mother, even though it had hurt like hell. So many times her heart had ached at knowing that they would never have the children they'd talked about together.

Now, looking into that gaping, six-year-old smile, she couldn't seem to stop the tide of emotions that washed over her—sorrow, envy and even an undeniable trace of anger that she'd been deprived all of this.

"Jo?"

Pete's voice cut through the anguish.

She forced a smile. "I'm sorry," she said, handing him back his wallet.

"No, I'm the one who's sorry," he said, his expression filled with regret. "I shouldn't have gotten into this with you."

"I asked," she reminded him.

"Still, I am sorry. It should never have been this way."

"No," she said softly, "it shouldn't have been." A lingering trace of anger crept into her voice. "Why *was* it, Pete? Why did it happen?"

He regarded her with a gaze filled with misery. "I wish I could tell you that it was all Kelsey's fault, that she set out to seduce me and trap me into marriage, but I have to be honest. It wasn't like that."

Jo almost wished she hadn't asked, but she needed to know. "Did you love her?"

"No," he said fiercely. "You were the one I loved. I promise you that. But you had gone home. Kelsey and I thought there was no harm to hanging out together, having a few beers. It wasn't about attraction or sex or even friendship, though I guess we were friends. We'd known each other since we were kids."

"Had you dated before?"

He shook his head. "No. It was all about being lonely, Jo. I missed you. And I was too damn young and stupid to realize that sleeping with some other woman wouldn't make that loneliness go away. It only happened once, because I knew right away that sex with anyone who wasn't you wasn't the answer."

"But once was enough," Jo said.

"Yeah, once was enough. It's an old story," Pete said. "When I found out Kelsey was pregnant, there was only one thing to do. I wasn't going to let my child grow up without a dad."

"The way you'd grown up," Jo said, understanding

at last. The marriage had been about far more than some moral obligation to Kelsey. It had always been about his son.

And knowing who Pete was and all the things that had shaped him into the man he'd become, she accepted that it couldn't have turned out any other way.

With that understanding came relief. She felt a weight lift from her heart. Forgiveness, which had always been an elusive concept to her, flooded in, and for the first time in seven years, she felt at peace.

"I should have told you all this back then," he said apologetically.

"I'm not sure it would have meant anything then," she admitted. "I was too hurt and too angry." She met his gaze. "I'm sorry the marriage didn't work out."

It seemed such a waste to her that it hadn't, that he'd sacrificed so much only to lose his son in the end, after all.

"So am I," he said.

It hurt to hear him say that. A part of her wished that he was glad to be rid of Kelsey, but it was a small, petty reaction. Again, he wouldn't be the man she'd loved if he'd been relieved that the marriage was over.

"I know it's none of my business, but what happened?" she asked him.

"I wasn't what she wanted," he said simply. "I never was."

The woman must be an idiot, Jo thought, but kept her reaction to herself. If Pete didn't cast aspersions on his ex-wife, she certainly wouldn't.

"You said they live in Richmond. That's not exactly around the corner. Do you get to spend much time with Davey?"

His eyes were filled with heartache when he replied, "Not nearly enough. We've worked out a schedule, and Kelsey usually sticks to it."

"Usually?"

"When she doesn't forget or make other plans—deliberately, more than likely."

"Does that happen often?"

"Often enough."

"That must be awful for you and your son."

He gave her a grim look. "I try not to let it be. I don't ever want Davey to be some pawn between his mother and me. That's why I didn't fight her for custody. He needs both of us. And as long as she's doing right by him, he'll never hear a harsh word about her from me."

"But if she's not living up to the agreement—" Jo began.

"I deal with her," Pete said. "We don't need the court involved."

Jo's respect for him grew. "You're an honorable man. I hope she knows what a treasure she threw away."

He laughed, but there was little humor in the sound. "I think she'd dispute that." He met her gaze. "Enough about me. Tell me about the man who didn't have the good sense to hang on to *you*."

She gave him a wry look. "You mean besides you."

He winced. "Ouch. I deserved that."

"You did," she agreed. "But I promise it'll be the last time I take potshots about the past. There's no point in living there."

"Amen to that," he replied. "Now stop avoiding the subject."

"The short version is that I came home and found him in bed with someone else," she said without emotion.

She had thought the image would be burned into her head forever, but ironically she couldn't picture it anymore. In fact, it hardly seemed to matter. Seeing Pete again had done that for her. Feeling the stir of those old emotions, knowing that the depth of what they'd once shared was so much more than anything she'd ever felt for her ex-fiancé, had put her heartache to rest. Since her love for Pete hadn't died nearly as quickly, she could only wonder if she'd ever loved James at all. Maybe that relationship had been on the rebound, despite the years it had taken for her to let another man into her heart.

Pete's gaze was steady and serious. "Want me to go beat him up for you?"

She returned his gaze with a solemn expression. "That's a lovely thought, but Ashley already offered. I turned her down."

"I'm meaner."

"You obviously don't know my big sister all that well."

"I saw her use a hammer," he said, then added with a grin, "She's a sissy."

Jo burst out laughing. "Please tell her that," she begged. "I want to be there."

"Think she'll pummel me to a bloody pulp?"

"I certainly think she'll try."

"It's good to hear you laugh, Jo," he said, his expression suddenly serious again.

"It's good to have something to laugh about," she admitted. "I was beginning to think I'd lost my sense of humor along with my fiancé."

"That would have been the real tragedy," Pete told her.

She lifted her gaze to his and felt the familiar stir of old desires. "It would have been, wouldn't it? I think I'm just beginning to see that."

"I could always make you laugh," he reminded her.

Because it hadn't always been that way, she reminded him. "You made me cry, too."

"And it's something I'll regret till my dying day," he told her.

Jo shook off the desire to weep one last time for all they'd lost. Instead, she met his gaze and lifted her glass of water in a solemn toast. "Here's to concentrating on the laughter from now on."

Pete lifted his bottle of beer and tapped it against the glass. "To laughter."

But even as they made the pact, Jo knew that there were no guarantees. The one thing certain about the future was its unpredictability. In fact, she would never in a million years have predicted that she would be sitting here in the kitchen at Rose Cottage sharing a meal with Pete again. Moreover, they'd found a way to laugh together again. That wasn't just totally unpredictable, it was a miracle.

But looking into Pete's eyes, feeling her heart begin to heal at long last, she realized that miracles truly could happen.

Chapter Six

Pete cursed himself six ways to Sunday all the way home from Jo's for having gotten drawn into even the briefest mention of his marriage. Up until tonight, he'd had a hard and fast rule: He didn't talk about it, not with anybody. What was the point, anyway? It was over and done with. Nobody needed to know the gory details. He'd always told himself he was keeping silent for his son's sake, but it was more than that. He didn't want anybody to know just how badly he'd screwed up.

Tonight he'd broken his own vow, and now he was regretting it. It would have been bad enough no matter whom he'd opened up to, but he sure as hell shouldn't have gotten into it with the woman who'd suffered because he hadn't known at twenty how to keep his pants zipped.

Then, again, maybe he had owed Jo that conversation. Maybe it was long overdue and damn the consequences to his pride. Possibly it would give her some satisfaction to know that he'd suffered too for the mistake he'd made. Maybe the humiliation of reliving it all would turn out to be worth it, if she'd been able to take some comfort in finally hearing the truth about his hasty, ill-advised marriage. Surely she couldn't think any worse of him than she did already. If she did, so be it. He could live with that, knowing that he'd finally been honest with her.

If they were ever going to have a second chance, Jo had to know the whole story. The fact that such a chance was even possible was a miracle, Pete realized. Mike had opened his eyes to that and made him see that it was a gift that shouldn't be tossed aside lightly. Since his attraction to Jo clearly hadn't died, he should be grateful for every second that gave him time to make amends and explore whether there was a chance for the two of them to recapture what they'd once had and build it into the dream they'd once shared.

Jo had been so damn innocent back then, so trusting. She'd believed in him—and in them—enough to give him not just her body, but her heart. He'd been way too careless with that gift. Because of that, he wasn't sure if he deserved a second chance, but obviously fate had other ideas since it had tossed them together now.

So far Jo had said nothing about how long she intended to stay, but he planned to use every minute to see if there was anything left of the feelings they'd once shared. One look at her had stirred something inside him, something he'd convinced himself was dead and buried. If he'd had to put a label on it, it wouldn't have been love exactly. No, it was more like hope.

When she'd been in his arms for those few brief moments, he thought he'd seen a fleeting spark of desire, a hint of longing in her eyes. He knew she'd responded to that kiss they'd shared. In fact, she'd looked as shaken by it as he had been. That could be the building block to something more. He just couldn't rush it. He had to keep in mind that she was in emotional pain herself. Her break-up was far fresher than his own. Taking advantage of that was out of the question.

No, he was older and, hopefully, wiser now. He was in it this time for the long haul. No mistakes. No blunders that would leave him racked with guilt and pain.

And with her entire family watching him like a hawk, he wasn't about to do anything that would give them cause to question his motives. Nope, he was going to be the perfect gentleman…even if it killed him.

Satisfied that he'd worked everything out—at least as much as he could control—he walked into his house with a lighter step. Immediately, he heard the phone ringing. By the time he snatched it up, the person had hung up, but the Richmond number on the caller ID told him it had been either Kelsey or his son. Though he had no particular desire to speak to his ex-wife, he couldn't take a chance that it had been Davey or that Kelsey was calling about his son. He dialed back immediately.

It was Davey who answered on the first ring. "Hello," he said, his voice quavering in an obviously frightened whisper.

All lingering thoughts of his unexpected evening

with Jo fled. Trying not to overreact, Pete kept his own tone light. "Hey, buddy, it's Dad. How's it shakin'?"

"How'd you know it was me who called?" his son asked, his voice filled with surprise and unmistakable relief.

"Caller ID. How come you didn't leave a message?"

"I dunno."

"You know it's always okay to call me, right?"

"I guess."

Something wasn't right. Davey loved to call, but he usually had a reason and was usually bubbling over with enthusiasm. Tonight, he was being surprisingly vague. Pete pressed gently for answers. "What's up, buddy? You okay?"

"I guess."

"Is everything going okay at school?"

"I guess."

"Is your mom around?"

Davey hesitated so long, Pete knew he'd finally hit on the problem. "Where's your mom?" he asked.

"She's on a date with that guy, the one I told you about," Davey said.

"Harrison something."

"Yeah."

"Is someone there with you?"

"I don't need a babysitter," Davey said bravely. "I'm almost seven."

Pete bit back a curse. Almost seven! Typical kid. He'd barely turned six, and he was already anxious to be a year older. Six was entirely too young for a kid to be on his own at night, especially in the city. So was seven, for that matter.

Down here was something else, but even here Pete would think long and hard before leaving his son rattling around in the house by himself. Kids needed supervision, whether they wanted it or not. His skin crawled when he thought of the mischief and danger the boy could have gotten into.

"How long has your mom been gone?" he asked, careful not to let Davey know just how furious he was.

"Not that long. A couple of hours, I guess."

"Did she leave you a number?"

"I've got her cell phone number," Davey said. "She promised to leave it on."

Pete's temper hit a boil. Despite everything he'd said to Jo earlier about trying to keep his relationship with Kelsey civil for Davey's sake, he'd just about had it with her irresponsibility. He obviously needed to have another talk with her about her neglectful approach to parenting. Until now, he'd tried just talking things out with her, but he was beginning to wonder if it wasn't time for him to press the issue in court. He hadn't fought her before, because he'd believed she was seriously trying to be a good mom. Lately, though, he didn't like some of the decisions she was making. Too often she was choosing her social life over their son's well-being.

"Dad, please don't be mad at Mom," Davey said, obviously sensing that he'd revealed too much. "I'm okay, really. I just thought maybe we could talk for a while."

"Of course we can talk," Pete said, trying to calm his fears. As long as Davey was on the phone with him, he'd know he was safe. He shrugged out of his jacket and settled into a chair. "Why don't you tell me what's happening at school these days?"

First grade apparently was more exciting than Pete remembered. He kept his son on the phone for an hour, listening to the increasingly carefree chatter about an awesome science project he'd seen.

"I could have done a really cool one that was better," Davey said. "But our teacher said we're too little. Isn't that dumb? What difference does it make how big we are?"

"None I can see," Pete agreed.

"Did I tell you I have a spelling test tomorrow? I'm going to ace it. I spelled all the words for Mom and she said I was perfect," Davey boasted.

"That's great," Pete told him. "Want to spell them for me?"

Davey giggled. "Dad, you're a lousy speller. You won't even know if I'm right."

"Hey, kid, mind your manners. I'm not that bad," he retorted.

"Mom says you are. She told me if I needed help with spelling, I'd better get it from her."

"Okay, maybe she has a point," Pete admitted. "But I'd like to hear the words anyway."

Davey spelled a couple, then yawned.

"You tired, buddy?"

"I guess."

"Then crawl into bed and get some sleep. Take the portable phone in with you. If you wake up and want to call me, it'll be right there, okay?"

"Okay."

"And don't answer the door, you hear me?"

"Dad, I know that," Davey said. "You've told me."

"Yeah, I guess I have," Pete said, grinning at his son's evident exasperation. "How about I come down this weekend and we can see about doing that science project you want to do? Nothing says you can't do it, even if it's not for school. We'll grab some lunch, too."

"Really?" Davey asked, then immediately tempered his excitement. "It's not a regular visit. I already looked on the calendar to see when you'd be coming again."

"I'll work it out with your mom. Now get some shut-eye, kid. Tomorrow's a school day."

"Bye, Dad. Love you."

"Love you more," Pete said, his heart aching.

He didn't waste so much as a split second on self-pity, though. He immediately punched in Kelsey's cell phone number. It took several rings before she picked up, and when she did, her voice was slurred. Even in that condition, he'd rather have her home with Davey than having the boy in the house all alone. Hell, maybe he should have called the cops instead and let the chips fall wherever they would, but he could only imagine the mess it would create with Davey caught smack in the middle. He'd probably end up in foster care before Pete could get it all straightened out. That wasn't an option, not even for a night.

"Get home right now," Pete said without ceremony. "And don't leave Davey there alone again or I'll haul you into court and take him away from you."

"What?" she asked, clearly fighting to grasp his words.

"I said to go home. I'll be calling there in fifteen minutes, and you'd better be there. If you're not, my next call will be to the police."

"You can't tell me what to do anymore," she protested.

"I think I just did," he responded. "When it comes to our son, I do have some say. If you don't believe it, try me."

"This is because you hate that I have someone new in my life and you don't," she said.

Pete clung to his patience by a thread. "I don't care who you date or what you do, unless and until it affects our son. Go home, Kelsey. You're down to twelve minutes to get there."

He slammed the phone down, waited the promised number of minutes with his eyes on the clock the whole time, then dialed the house. Kelsey picked up at once.

"Don't ever do that to me again," she said tightly. "You embarrassed me with a friend."

"That's nothing to what I'm likely to do if I find out you've ever left that boy in the house alone again. I don't care if it's day or night—he's too young to be there by himself. I've warned you before, and I'm beginning to think it fell on deaf ears."

"Okay, okay, I hear you, but I think you're getting worked up over nothing. Davey's a very responsible kid."

"He's six, dammit. What's he going to do if there's an emergency?"

"He knows how to call 911."

"Fat lot of good that will do him if the house is on fire and he can't get to a phone."

"Dammit, Pete, you're acting crazy," she said in a tone that was all bluster. "Davey is perfectly fine. How'd you find out he was here alone anyway?"

"He called me," he said. "And don't even think about taking this out on him. He called because he was scared. He did exactly the right thing."

"He's sound asleep," she protested, sounding a bit more uncertain. "How scared could he have been?"

"Scared enough to call me and spend an hour on the phone just to have a little company."

She didn't seem to have an answer to that.

"Okay, here's the deal. I'm coming down on Saturday," Pete informed her without leaving any room for argument. "I promised him we'd go out for the day."

"But—"

"Don't even think about trying to stop me, Kelsey."

"Fine. Whatever."

"Think of it this way. You can finish up your hot date, while I've got our son covered."

He slammed the phone down, satisfied that Davey was safe enough at least for tonight.

Then he grabbed a beer from the fridge, but before he'd taken the first sip, he dumped it down the drain. Getting stinking drunk wasn't the solution. It hadn't worked when his marriage was crumbling. It wouldn't work now.

The only thing that might marginally improve his mood would be seeing Jo, but he couldn't go barging in over there again tonight. And this definitely wasn't a problem he could dump on her shoulders. She didn't deserve getting dragged into this quagmire. It would just be rubbing salt in an old wound.

It was only a few hours till morning, though. He could make it till then. He'd pick up some of those blueberry doughnuts she used to love and be on her doorstep right after dawn. Maybe then this ache in the region of his heart would go away. And those doughnuts might earn him enough goodwill that he could sneak in another of those mind-blowing kisses.

He grinned for the first time since he'd called Davey. Now *that,* he thought, was something to look forward to.

* * *

Jo was still half-asleep when she heard Pete outside. She squinted at the clock and saw that it was barely six-thirty. She fell back against the pillows with a moan. It wasn't even daylight yet, but he was already hammering the heck out of something. She was surprised he could even see.

That didn't seem to be stopping him, though. Since the racket showed no sign of lessening, she dragged herself up and into the bathroom. She took a quick shower, pulled on jeans and a heavy knit sweater, ran a comb through her damp hair and walked downstairs in search of her shoes and socks. The minute she switched on the downstairs lights, Pete knocked on the door, then stuck his head in.

"You awake?"

Jo laughed at the ridiculous question. "As if anyone could sleep with all that racket you were making. What on earth were you doing?"

"Starting on the porch."

"In the dark?"

"I could see well enough." He surveyed her, then grinned. "You're not much of a morning person, are you?"

"I am when I have to be."

He dangled a bag in front of her. "Will this help?"

She sniffed and immediately smelled the heavenly aroma of sugar and blueberries. "Oh, my God," she said, snatching the bag away from him and burying her face inside. "I can't believe the bakery is still making these."

"Yes, and they're fresh from the oven. I stopped by on my way over here and wheedled a few out of Helen. She remembered how you loved them."

"You're a saint."

"Hardly, but am I at least forgiven for dragging you out of bed?"

"That depends." She peered inside the bag again and counted. "A half dozen," she said with a blissful sigh. "You're definitely forgiven." She grinned at him. "For waking me, anyway."

"You gonna share?"

"Do I have to?"

Pete chuckled. "No, but it's a darn good thing I bought a couple for myself."

She took out the first one, slowly savored the aroma of sugar and blueberries, then bit into it. The sugar rush went straight to her brain. She'd never tasted anything quite like these and she'd been looking for years.

"Oh, my," she murmured after the first bite. "These are heaven."

"Does your sister the gourmet chef know that the only food you really crave in life is a blueberry doughnut?"

Jo nodded. "It pains her greatly. She even tried to learn to make them, but good as she is, hers never measured up. How did Helen remember that I love these? It's been years since I've been in there."

"Hey," he protested. "Don't I get some of the credit?"

She chuckled. "Yes. I thought I'd already praised you. How did *you* remember that this was my favorite breakfast in the whole world?"

"You'd be surprised at the things I remember," he said in a way that made her heart skitter crazily.

It was way too early in the morning to go there. "Pete, don't say things like that," she pleaded, as if that would stop the sizzle in the air between them.

"Why not? It's true. I remember everything about that summer." He stepped closer and gazed into her eyes. "I remember the way you looked first thing in the morning, all dewy-eyed and fresh. You were no better at crawling out of bed early back then, either." He touched a finger to her lips. "And I remember how your lips tasted of blueberries and sugar. I was addicted to that taste for years. Couldn't get it out of my head, but just eating doughnuts wasn't enough. I kept telling Helen she was leaving something out, till I realized that what I needed was you. You were the missing ingredient."

He touched his mouth to hers and skimmed his tongue along the seam. Jo felt the earth shift beneath her feet.

"Pete," she protested, but without much energy.

"What, Jo?"

"We can't go back," she whispered, even though she couldn't seem to tear her gaze away. "Too much has happened. And if we dredge it all up, it'll make it impossible for me to work with you."

"So we should pretend it never happened?" he asked incredulously.

She drew in a deep breath and said firmly, "I think that's best."

"I think it's impossible."

So did she, if she were being honest. She'd just planned to push down the old feelings in the vague hope that all the new ones would vanish as well. Her reaction to this morning's treat proved that old and new were bound to be all tangled together.

"How about a compromise? I won't talk about the past if you won't," she said. "We don't have to pretend it didn't happen. We just won't talk it to death. We pretty well covered it last night anyway."

He didn't look convinced. "Then there's nothing more you think we need to say?" he asked.

"Nothing," she said staunchly.

He looked as if he wanted to debate the point, but he finally nodded. "Okay, I can ignore it, if you can." He turned away from her, hands shoved in his pockets. "I'm going to spend another hour working on the porch and then we can go over to the house I was telling you about. Will you be ready?"

She hated the sudden distance in his voice, as if they were little more than colleagues…or strangers. But she was the one who'd insisted it be this way, so how could she complain?

"I'll be ready," she told him. "I just need to hunt down my shoes and socks."

He left the kitchen, taking the life from the room when he went. She sagged into a chair and absentmindedly picked up another doughnut. After one bite, though, she realized that she wasn't really tasting it and put it aside. Why waste something so delicious?

She sipped her coffee, but it left a bitter aftertaste in her mouth. Acknowledging that her conversation with Pete had pretty much ruined a morning that had started out brightly, she scowled in the direction of the porch where he was hammering away again.

She didn't want it to be like this. Last night, things had felt natural, comfortable. Today, the air was filled with tension, and it was all her fault. What had she been thinking with her stupid ground rules? She was smart enough to know that as soon as a topic or a person was declared off-limits, it became huge, far more important than it otherwise might have been. Now the past and their old feelings for each other loomed between them.

She noticed that Pete had left his cup of coffee on the table and made a decision. She freshened it up, then carried it outside and handed it to him silently.

He watched her warily. "Thanks."

"You're welcome." She swallowed hard. "I'm sorry."

"For?"

"Being a first-class idiot."

He grinned and the tension vanished. "You? Never. You were always the smartest girl I knew."

"Maybe I grew into being dumb," she said, not entirely in jest. "I know we can't pretend that the past never happened. Last night we promised to concentrate on laughing again. Can we still do that?"

"Fine with me." He studied her over the rim of the cup, waiting. Finally, he said, "So, know any good jokes?"

She grinned. "Not a one."

"Me, either—at least none I can tell to a lady."

She shrugged. "Just as well. I'm freezing. I'll go back inside. I just wanted to, you know, settle things, make them okay again."

He tucked a finger under her chin. "Things are fine."

She felt the smile build from somewhere deep inside. "Good to know."

"Skedaddle, woman. You're distracting me."

She gave him one last look before she went back inside. He winked at her, and her heart did a predictable somersault.

Inside, she asked herself why it was so important to

her that she and Pete be friends again. It was only opening the door to more potential heartache. She knew it
wasn't because he'd offered her work. She could have
managed for a bit without those two jobs he'd discussed
with her. Nor was it because she didn't like being on the
outs with anyone.

No, this was very personal. It was about her relationship with Pete—the one they'd had and the one she had
a terrifying hunch that she wanted again.

Chapter Seven

Pete was still feeling completely off-kilter when he stopped work on the porch and told Jo it was time to drive over to the job site. He'd come damn close to dragging her into his arms after that kiss earlier, but he'd known he wouldn't be content with a few more kisses. Better to keep some distance between them. Jo needed to get used to the idea of being around him again, and rattling her was no way to accomplish that.

Of course, it was fairly difficult to get too much distance between them in the cab of a pickup. He could smell that familiar, old-fashioned scent she'd always worn, something light and flowery. It had always reminded him of her grandmother's garden. For a long time he hadn't been able to smell a rose without being transported to Rose Cottage. When Kelsey had wanted to put rose bushes all around their house, he'd vehemently protested. To Pete's relief, she'd grudgingly substituted a hodgepodge of lilacs, hydrangeas and azaleas, which she'd then neglected.

He'd eventually come to hate that little house with its haphazard, struggling garden. No more than an aging beach cottage, it was cramped and filled with reminders of all the mistakes he'd ever made. He'd kept the roof solid and the exterior painted, but he'd been so busy building his business, he hadn't had the time or money to invest in any of the extras that would have made it more livable. If the people whose homes he'd built in recent years had ever seen where he lived, he wasn't sure they would be trusting him with their dream homes.

He was about to change that, though. One of the places he wanted Jo to landscape was going to be his. He hadn't told her that. He wasn't sure why, except that he hadn't decided which house to keep just yet. He was half hoping that her reaction would help him decide. Maybe he even feared she'd back out of the job if she thought he was the client she was ultimately going to have to please. After all, he'd pretty much agreed to give her carte blanche to landscape the places for some anonymous buyers who'd hopefully come along in the spring.

They rode the few miles to the first house in silence. That was another thing he'd always loved about Jo. She'd never felt the need to fill every minute with chatter. It was yet another way in which Kelsey had fallen short by comparison. Kelsey couldn't keep quiet for ten minutes if her life depended on it. It had driven him nuts. A million other traits had driven him just as crazy, but the one positive—his son—had made him struggle to ignore the rest.

When he turned onto the dirt road that led to the first Cape Cod-style house with its soft gray shingles and white trim, he slanted a look at Jo. She was sitting on the edge of the seat, her eyes filled with anticipation. When the house finally came into view, she gasped.

"Oh, Pete, it's absolutely beautiful." She turned to him with shining eyes. "Can I see the inside?"

He grinned. "You planning to landscape in there, too?"

"Very funny." She gave him a pleading look. "Please?"

He laughed, taking pleasure in her delight. "Of course you can see the inside. It's still a work in progress. A lot of the finishing touches won't be done until March or so. The real estate market around here kicks into high gear in April, so I'm not rushing to complete it too much ahead of that."

"That's okay, I can use my imagination."

The minute he pulled to a stop, she leaped eagerly from the truck without waiting for his assistance. She was halfway to the front door by the time he caught up with her.

"You're awfully eager," he teased. "Or are you just cold?"

"Eager," she said without hesitation as she crossed the sweeping porch and waited for him. "Come on, slowpoke. Open up."

Pete unlocked the front door, then stepped aside and waited, his heart admittedly in his throat.

"Oh, my," Jo murmured as she stepped into the foyer with its shining hardwood floors and a skylight that sent sunlight cascading over everything, turning the oak to a golden hue. "It's beautiful."

She walked through the downstairs rooms almost reverently, expressing delight with the windows, the fireplace, the crown molding, the French doors in the dining room that led to a soft pink brick patio, the bright kitchen with its view of the Chesapeake Bay from the window that would eventually be over the sink as well as from the bay windows around the built-in breakfast nook that had been framed in, but not completed.

"It's charming," she said over and over. "Absolutely perfect." She grinned at him. "You have incredible taste. What kind of cabinets will you have in here?"

"White with glass doors. I want to use the old-fashioned glass that has a few bubbles and ripples in it, so the place will look as though it has some age to it. What do you think?"

"I think that's exactly right," she said. "Every detail is just what I would have chosen."

Pete had to bite back the desire to tell her that she was the one who'd inspired him. He couldn't remind her that they'd built this same dream house on a dozen different occasions over that incredible summer. It hurt in some way he couldn't name that she didn't seem to share that memory, that she wasn't recognizing the details he'd worked to get just right.

"How many bedrooms upstairs?" she asked.

"Five, including the master suite. Most of the work that's left is up there and here in the kitchen."

"I still want to go up. May I?"

"Of course."

This time he let her go alone. He stood at the kitchen

window and stared out at the view, remembering how careful he'd been to be sure it was at exactly the right angle to capture the sunlight on the bay in the morning. He heard Jo's footsteps going from room to room, even heard the occasional exclamation and tried to guess what she was seeing. Her delight filled his heart with satisfaction and, maybe just a little, with regret.

This house could have been theirs. They could have finalized every detail together, but instead it had all been up to him. It wasn't enough that he knew her so well that he'd pleased her anyway. The real joy would have come in the sharing, in the excursions to look at everything from faucets to ceiling fans and flooring.

Still, he couldn't deny that it felt good knowing that he'd built something she liked. He could hardly wait to see how she reacted to the second house. It was ironic given how long they'd been apart, but he'd actually felt as if she were with him as he'd designed and built it.

"Hey, it's cold in here," he finally hollered. "Are you ever going to get down here and do the job I hired you for?"

She danced down the steps, her cheeks glowing. "That's some tub you installed in the master suite," she teased him.

"Big enough for two," he confirmed.

"Lucky couple."

He grinned. "Indeed. Ready to look around outside?"

"I'll need to get my notepad from the truck so I can make a few sketches and jot down my ideas."

Pete nodded. "I'll meet you out by the oak tree in back. Wait till you see it in the spring and next fall. It's spectacular."

Some of the light in her eyes died. "I'll have to take

your word for it," she said. "I'll probably be back in Boston by then, but I'm glad you saved it. Too many builders just slash down everything in sight these days."

"There was no way I'd cut this down. I kept imagining a swing hanging from its branches or a tree house built way up high. Besides, it adds to the feeling that this place is substantial. Even makes it feel as if it's been around for a while."

To his astonishment, she stood on tiptoe and planted an impulsive kiss on his cheek. "Nice to see you getting all sentimental about a tree."

She was gone before he could react. He wandered around back and leaned against the massive trunk of the saved oak that had earned him an unexpected kiss. He nudged it with an elbow. "Thanks," he murmured, then felt like an idiot.

Even with the sun shining brightly, the air off the water was frigid. Pete shivered as he waited for Jo to join him. When she didn't appear after several minutes, he went looking for her. He found her by his truck, her pad resting on the hood as she made some sketches, her pencil flying over the page. He went up to peer over her shoulder.

There, in front of his eyes, was a climbing rose bush creeping up to the porch railing. A pond was taking shape off to one side, surrounded by some sort of flowering bushes. She blinked and looked up at him.

"Where'd you come from?"

"Around back, where I was waiting for you."

"Sorry," she said, but with little real repentance. "Inspiration struck and I wanted to get it down on paper. I'm thinking a wildflower garden over here with a birdbath. It will draw butterflies and birds, so people sitting on the porch will be able to watch them. What do you think?"

"People actually sit around and watch birds?"

She laughed. "We used to."

He thought back and recalled how they'd been end-lessly entertained by the turf wars over her grand-mother's birdbath and the hummingbird feeder. "I'd forgotten," he admitted. "Where's the hummingbird feeder going?"

"With the plants I have in mind, you won't need one. They'll be drawn to the flowers."

"You know, if you're going to go into this much de-tail all around the yard, we'd better come back another day. I don't want you to freeze to death out here. How about grabbing some lunch while we warm up a bit, then taking a quick look at the other place?"

She waved off the question, her attention back on the page. She was sketching something else, some sort of arbor.

"What's that?" he asked.

"Wisteria. This place cries out for a white picket fence and an arbor. It'll give it a nice, old-fashioned touch."

"If you say so. Now, how about lunch?" he prod-ded again.

"Since I think my fingers are turning into blocks of ice, lunch sounds good."

Pete impulsively clasped her hands in his and rubbed them, then kissed the tips of her fingers. She gave him a startled look, but then a slow smile crept across her face.

"Is this one of those perks that comes with the job?" she asked.

"I'll even put it in the contract, if you want me to."

She nodded slowly. "Just be sure you make it an exclusive."

Pete chuckled. "Believe me, you're the only person who works for me whose hands aren't scarred up and calloused. This treatment is definitely reserved for you."

As if the whole exchange had suddenly made her nervous, she withdrew her hands and tucked them in her pockets. She headed around to the passenger door of the truck, then shot one last grin over her shoulder. "I'll want that in writing."

Pete laughed. "Done, darlin'."

She was playing with fire, Jo warned herself as she sipped the hot seafood chowder she'd ordered for lunch. Something daring had crept over her back at the job site and she hadn't been able to help herself, but she could not keep tossing out innuendoes and letting Pete steal kisses. Not only was it unprofessional, it was dangerous. For hours now her blood had been humming through her veins the way it had that long-ago summer. She'd felt every bit as giddy and impulsive as the schoolgirl she'd been back then, too.

And look what had happened, she reminded herself sternly.

She glanced across the table and realized Pete's gaze was resting on her. "What?" she asked.

"You look as if you're giving yourself a very stern lecture," he teased.

"I am," she admitted.

"About?"

"You."

"Oh?"

"Just reminding myself that you're a client."

Something flickered in his eyes, something she couldn't really interpret. Hurt, maybe.

"I thought we were more than that, Jo," he said quietly. "I thought we were friends."

"We *were* friends," she agreed. "In fact, we *were* even more than that. You changed everything. I can't let myself forget that."

"Yeah, I suppose you're right. Trust doesn't come easily once it's been destroyed. I guess I need to remember that, too." He glanced at her bowl. "You finished? We should probably get going."

Sorry that she'd spoiled the easygoing mood between them yet again, Jo merely nodded. It was just as well. They'd been getting too comfortable together...again.

Pete threw a couple of ones on the table, then paid the check. "Are you up for seeing the other house?"

"Of course," she said, not even trying to hide her eagerness. If it was anything at all like the first one, she was going to love it.

A few minutes later, Pete turned off the main road and cut through a densely wooded lot. When they finally emerged into a clearing, Jo felt her heart begin to pound. She recognized this house as if she'd seen it a thousand times before. In a way she had, because she and Pete had talked about it so often.

She'd had a similar reaction to the first house, but not like this. This morning, certain touches had seemed vaguely familiar, like a distant memory stirring but not quite gelling. Her reaction to this house, though, was intense and instantaneous. There was no mistaking that this was their dream house.

Unlike the first one, this was all on one floor, sprawling over the waterfront land to take advantage of every view, every breeze. Even from where they sat, she could see through one set of French doors straight through the house to another set that faced the Chesapeake. She already knew there would be ceiling fans in every room, that the porch facing the water would have Victorian trim and railings meant to hold flower boxes spilling over with color.

Despite its obvious size, it somehow captured the feeling of a seaside cottage, something cozy and filled with light and the scent of salt air. She was willing to bet that the master suite would be at one end with rooms for kids and guests at the other, giving the owners privacy even when the house was overrun with family or company.

Despite all her earlier admonitions, she turned to Pete with her heart in her throat. "You built our house," she said softly. "Just the way we talked about."

Hands stuffed in his pockets, he nodded. "I tried."

"But why? And how can you turn around and sell it?"

He looked vaguely embarrassed, which in itself was a shock.

Pete never looked anything other than confident.

"In a weird way, it started out as punishment, sort of a torment," he admitted, "but in the end it made me feel close to you again. I brought in plumbers and electricians, but all the rest I did myself. I started it right after my divorce became final."

"Then I'll ask again—how can you sell it?"

"I'm not going to," he said, as if he'd just reached a decision. "I'm going to live here."

"But you told me before you intended to sell both of these houses."

"I think I might have, if you hadn't reacted the way you did just now. The minute I saw your face, I knew I couldn't part with this one, after all." His gaze lingered on hers. "Want to see the inside?"

"Yes," she said at once, then, "No."

He regarded her with amusement. "Which is it?"

"I'm not sure. I think I'm afraid to see the inside."

"Afraid I've gotten it wrong?" he asked.

"No. I'm terrified you've gotten it exactly right," she confessed.

"Would that be so awful?"

Yes, Jo thought to herself. Because Pete would live here without her.

Aloud, she forced herself to say, "No, I suppose not."

He hopped out of the truck and went around to open her door. When he held out his hand, she took it, then reluctantly stepped down.

At the front door, she hesitated again. She lifted her gaze to meet his. "You know if I walk through this door and fall in love, there's going to be a problem, don't you?"

He looked perplexed. "What sort of problem?"

"You're going to have to fight me to keep this place."

Pete laughed, then sobered when he apparently realized she was at least halfway serious.

He shrugged. "There's an easy solution to that, you know. You can just move in here with me."

Even though his tone was light, Jo's heart tumbled straight to her toes. The suggestion was too damn tempting. "You know that's not possible," she said at once, a reminder meant as much for her as for him.

"Of course, it is," he said just as readily, then winked at her. "But I've got another few weeks' worth of work to do. You have time to decide."

But when the door swung open and Jo stepped through, she knew it wouldn't take nearly that long. She felt as if she'd just come home.

"He's gotten every single detail exactly right," Jo complained to her sisters when they stopped by later that evening.

"And that's a bad thing?" Melanie asked cautiously, clearly not quite certain what to make of Jo's mood.

"Yes, dammit. I am not supposed to fall in love with a house here, but I have to tell you, I want that house."

Ashley and Maggie exchanged a grin. "Maybe he'll sell it to you," Ashley suggested. "Building and selling houses is what he does, after all."

"And what will I use to buy it? I don't have any savings, at least not enough to put a down payment on that house."

"What was he going to ask for it?"

"I have no idea, but with real estate booming here and that incredible water view, it's got to be at least half a million. Maybe more. That's way out of my league," Jo said with regret.

"But you do want it?" Ashley persisted. "It's more than sentiment talking?"

"Absolutely," she insisted, knowing it was impulsive and irrational and completely out of character, especially since until a couple of hours ago she'd had every intention of going back to Boston. "The minute I stepped inside, I knew that house was mine."

"Unfortunately, Pete seems to be thinking of it as his," Melanie reminded her.

Jo frowned. "Don't you think I know that? He was grinning like a fool when he saw me drooling over the place. Now he knows he has leverage. He has something I want, and he knows I'll do just about anything to get it."

For the first time since they'd started talking about the house, Ashley looked alarmed. "What do you mean by anything?"

Jo scowled at her. "I'm not going to murder the man in his sleep, if that's what you're worried about. I'll probably be doing free landscaping design for him till my dying day trying to persuade him to sell me the house."

"Actually I wasn't worried so much about murder. I could defend you against that," Ashley said with a dismissive wave of her hand. "I'm more concerned that you're going to get mixed up with a man you barely know just because he happened to build your dream house."

Jo stared at her blankly, then realized that none of her sisters had a clue that Pete had actually built the house because of her. If they knew her history with Pete, Ashley's mild worry would turn into utter panic. Jo should have kept her mouth shut about this whole stupid mess. It wasn't as if she could have the house, after all. It was just that they'd arrived while her desire for the place was still fresh. She hadn't been able to stop talking about the house from the moment they'd arrived.

"Me getting mixed up with Pete is not an issue," she

assured her sister. "Let's forget about the house. I can't have it, and that's that. I shouldn't have brought it up."

"But you did, and you obviously feel passionately about it," Ashley said. "Let's get practical. Maybe Pete will build you another house just like it, maybe something on a smaller scale and more affordable."

"It wouldn't be the same," Jo said wistfully.

"Come on, Jo. That's a great idea," Melanie enthused. "If you go into partnership with Mike, you'll have the money for a down payment in no time. Heck, maybe you can even barter a few jobs with Pete to get the rest."

Jo knew it was ridiculous, but she didn't want an exact replica. She wanted this one, at least in part because she knew she'd been on Pete's mind when he'd designed and built it.

But it was out of the question, and that was the end of it.

"Come on, guys, I never should have gotten into this. You just caught me in a weak moment. Let's talk about something else."

"Such as?" Maggie asked.

Though she tried desperately, Jo couldn't think of an alternative topic. Images of the house kept flashing in her mind. She'd been mentally decorating the place ever since she'd seen it. There would be lots of blue-striped cushions and chintz, and old-fashioned wicker furniture for the porch.

"There you go," Ashley said, when it was clear Jo was stumped for another subject. "This is the only thing that really matters to you. Let's come up with a plan."

Jo studied her with a narrowed gaze. "What kind of plan?"

"To get that house away from Pete, of course."

"Feminine wiles," Melanie said at once, only to draw scowls from the rest of them. "Hey, it works. Isn't that all that matters?"

"No, it is not," Jo said firmly. She couldn't see herself seducing the house away from Pete. That would just complicate an already tricky situation. In fact, he'd probably be delighted to have her try. He had invited her to move in, after all. Even if the offer had been made in jest, she knew he'd be thrilled if she took him up on it. Only she knew how impossible that was. She was not putting her heart at risk, even for the home she'd always wanted.

"Money talks," Ashley said, shooting a daunting look at Melanie. "Let's see what kind of down payment we can scrape together and make the man an offer he can't refuse."

"It's not about the money," Jo assured her. "Pete loves this house as much as I do."

"Men don't fall in love with houses. They want a roof over their heads," Ashley scoffed.

"Excuse me," Jo protested. "But don't you think it might be different with Pete? He builds houses for a living. They have to mean something to him for him to be so good at it."

Melanie regarded her curiously. "You're certainly quick to jump to his defense. And you seem to understand what makes him tick. How well have you gotten to know him?"

"Oh, for pity's sake," Jo muttered. "You all are impossible. It's about the house, not Pete. How did we get off track?"

"I thought it was because the two were so inter-twined," Ashley said, a smug expression on her face.

Jo saw she was not going to win an argument with this crowd, not without divulging a whole lot more than she wanted to about her history with Pete.

"How about some ice cream?" she asked cheerfully. "I have hot fudge sauce."

"It's thirty degrees outside and you want ice cream?" Ashley asked.

"With *hot* fudge sauce," Jo said. "That makes all the difference."

"Count me in," Melanie said at once.

"Me, too," Maggie agreed,

Ashley clearly wasn't going to be so easily dis-tracted, but when she opened her mouth, Maggie frowned at her, and she clamped her lips together.

"Ashley will have ice cream, too," Maggie said with a grin.

"Yes, I will," Ashley said primly. "And then we'll get back to Pete."

Jo sighed, but she dished out the ice cream and prayed she could get them all out of the house before her big sister made good on her promise.

Chapter Eight

It was Friday before Pete came around to Rose Cottage again. Despite her desire to keep her emotions in check where he was concerned, Jo realized she'd missed him. She was too honest not to admit that, at least to herself. She told herself it was merely because she was anxious to look for some chink in his determination to keep that house. She also told herself that her long-held hurt and anger over his betrayal were as strong as they'd ever been. They had to be.

Maybe so, she admitted ruefully, but she couldn't seem to stay away from him. He was on the porch, hammering away, when she took him a mug of steaming coffee.

"How's it going?" she asked as she handed it to him.

He paused, took a cautious sip of the coffee, then surveyed what he'd accomplished. The new tongue-and-groove flooring was about halfway finished. "It would move a lot faster if I weren't tied up on so many other jobs right now."

"There's no rush," Jo assured him. "Have you had time to do any work on your two spec houses since we went by there the other day?" She'd deliberately chosen to refer to them as "spec houses" in order to minimize the attachment they both clearly felt, at least to the one.

He grinned, as if he understood her ploy. "I haven't had much time. I usually work over there on the weekends, but that's out this weekend."

"Oh?"

"I need to go down to Richmond Saturday morning to see Davey," he said, then studied her as if to see if the reference to his son was upsetting.

Jo worked to keep her expression neutral so he'd continue. Eventually, he shrugged.

"Something came up the other night," he said. "I promised him I'd get down there to spend some time with him."

Envy streaked through Jo, though she didn't pause to define the cause. "The two of you have big plans then?" she asked.

"Any time I get to spend with my son is a big deal," he said at once, a surprising edge in his voice.

"Well, of course, I just meant—"

He cut her off. "I know what you meant. I'm sorry. Look, I won't bore you with the details, but things got a little tense between Kelsey and me the other night. I need to straighten some things out with her. I'm not looking forward to it, and I really don't want to talk about it, especially not with you. I won't drag you into the middle of this. It's not fair."

"You don't get to decide what's fair," she retorted. "Maybe I could offer a woman's perspective."

"No," he said flatly.

There was a finality in his voice that told Jo he wouldn't appreciate her prying any more deeply into what had happened. She bit her tongue and deliberately changed the subject.

"Since you won't be around, do you mind if I go over to the houses tomorrow and do some more sketches?" she asked.

"Of course not. That's what I hired you for."

She grinned at him. "You haven't actually hired me yet. Maybe we ought to talk about the exorbitant rates I charge for my expertise before we go any further."

"Whatever your going rate is, I'll pay it," he said without hesitation. "I want the landscaping done right. Mike says you can handle it, and that's good enough for me. Besides, I saw those preliminary sketches you did in just a few minutes the other day. I know you've got a feel for these houses."

"I'm glad you're pleased, but I still think we ought to talk about my fee," she said. "I don't want there to be any problems when I turn in the bill. This is a professional thing, Pete. It doesn't have anything to do with, well, us. You'd write up a contract with Mike, wouldn't you?"

"Okay, you're right. Why don't you put something down on paper, and I'll come inside in a half hour or so and sign it?"

Jo nodded. "Perfect."

He regarded her with amusement. "And just so you know, I'm going to read the fine print, darlin'. I didn't miss the gleam in your eyes when we left that second house the other day. I don't want you sneaking in some deal to get that house away from me."

Jo laughed. "Never crossed my mind."

"Yeah, right," he said skeptically. "I know how your mind works, but just so you know, there's only one way you're ever moving into that house and it's with me."

She frowned at him. "Be careful. You saw how much I love that place. I might take you up on that, and then where would you be?"

"In heaven," he retorted lightly. "Or the closest thing to it."

The expression in his eyes was just serious enough to make her tremble. "Pete," she whispered in what sounded more like a plea than a protest.

A wicked grin spread across his face. "Don't panic, Jo. I'm not going to push you into anything you don't want to do."

But, of course, that was precisely the problem. Despite all the stern lectures, despite her best intentions, this was something she was starting to *want,* desperately in fact. Not just that house, but Pete. He wasn't just a rebound romance, despite what she'd told him. She realized now that he was the only man she'd ever truly loved. It should have scared her to death, but with every day that passed she was growing more at peace with that knowledge.

Pete finished up as much work on the porch as he could before dusk fell, then went inside Rose Cottage. Jo was sitting at the kitchen table, still looking rattled by their earlier exchange. He could relate to the feeling.

He'd been in a state of perpetual turmoil ever since she'd opened the front door the first night he'd come by about fixing up the porch. The unexpected wonder of seeing her then was still with him.

"Penny for your thoughts," he said when she looked up at him with a startled expression as if she hadn't been expecting him.

"My going rate's a lot higher than that," she said, dragging her attention back from wherever it had wandered.

He picked up the piece of paper on the table. "I assume our deal is all spelled out on here."

She nodded. "I gave you a break from what I'd charge in Boston."

Without even looking at the paper, Pete frowned at her. "I don't want a break."

Her chin came up. "Well, I gave you one anyway."

He tossed the paper on the table. "Take it back."

"I most certainly will not. Stop being so blasted stubborn. You haven't even looked at it." She handed it right back to him. "See? It's not like I'm going to go broke."

It was a nice round number, but it wasn't enough. "Fair is fair, Jo. This isn't even half as high as what Mike would charge me."

She faltered at that. "Really?"

"Really," he assured her. "If you won't make the change, I will." He picked up the contract, filled in a new set of numbers, then scrawled his signature across the bottom.

"This is more like it," he said as he handed it back to her.

She frowned as she read it. "You can't be serious."

"Oh, but I am. Ask Mike. He tells me all the time that he's being conservative, too."

There was a spark in her eyes he couldn't quite interpret,

"That lowdown scumbag," she muttered under her breath, her gaze still on the paper.

Puzzled by her reaction, he stared at her. "Who's a scumbag? Mike?"

"No, of course not," she said. "My boss in Boston. Everyone told me he was a tightwad, but I'm just beginning to see how much he was probably making, thanks to me."

"Seems to me that's a good reason not to go back there," Pete said, then added casually, "Assuming you need one."

"I might go back to Boston, but I sure as hell won't be working for him again," she said fiercely.

Pete laughed at her infuriated tone. "Maybe I ought to call Mike right now and tell him this might be a good time to sign you up for a partnership."

She gave him a sly look. "It might be, if I had the perfect place to live."

He chuckled, "Very clever, but you have Rose Cottage. There's nothing wrong with this place that a little loving attention won't fix right up. Your sisters have already done a lot to whip it back into shape. The foundation and roof are solid. The porch is the last big investment you'll be making."

"But there's an even more perfect place a few miles from here," she told him.

He regarded her innocently. "But the price is way too high for you, isn't that what you've been telling me? And it's awfully big for one person living all alone."

"Give me a price in dollars and cents, and there might be bargaining room," she countered.

"There's lots more to life than money," he reminded her.

"That's not what you used to say," Jo replied. "When I knew you, all you could think about was getting your business started and making a name for yourself. You were very ambitious."

"But now that I've done that, I see the flaw in my thinking," Pete confessed. "None of it matters a damn, if there's no one around to share it."

Jo met his gaze and released a sigh. "I can't argue with that," she said. She got to her feet and opened the refrigerator door. "Can you stay for dinner?"

Pete walked over behind her and pushed the door closed. "Jo?"

When she turned to face him, tears were glistening on her cheeks.

"What is it?" he asked, rubbing the pad of his thumb across the damp, silky skin. He had to fight the desire to swoop in and claim her lips.

"Nothing," she insisted, trying to duck under his arm.

Pete dropped a hand on her shoulder and kept her in place. "Talk to me," he pleaded. "What did I say to upset you?"

"It wasn't you," she insisted. "I'm just an idiot."

"Never."

"I am. I'm always wanting something I can't have or something that's wrong for me."

"Such as?"

Her gaze met his, then darted away.

"There's nothing you can't say to me," he told her. "Nothing. What is it you can't have that you want?"

A spark of anger flickered in her eyes as she faced him. "I wanted you once," she said with such quiet regret that it made Pete's heart twist. "And I wanted James, at least till I figured out what a dope he was."

"Anything else?"

Her lips curved slightly. "I want that house."

Pete cupped her chin in his hands and looked into her eyes. "It was made for you," he said quietly.

Surprise lit her eyes. "You'll sell it to me?"

Maybe he should. It was obvious the place meant something to her, perhaps even more than it meant to him, though he didn't see how that was possible. But that house was the one thing that might keep the door open for him to get back into her life. He couldn't relinquish it too easily.

"Sorry," he said. "I can't sell it to you."

The excitement in her eyes died. "Can't or won't?"

"Doesn't matter. The house is mine."

"I could hate you for the ten seconds when you let me get my hopes up," she muttered.

"Just add it to the list," he advised. "You have bigger reasons to hate me."

"But I've been working on forgiving you for those," she said.

He grinned. "How's that going?"

"Not half as well as it was about five minutes ago," she replied.

"I figured as much," he said, then dropped that kiss on her lips after all. "I think I'll skip dinner tonight. We both have a lot of thinking to do. I'll see you when I get back."

"Maybe you will, maybe you won't," she said airily.

Pete picked the contract off the table and waved it

under her nose. "This says I will. I know you'd never go back on your word."

"Why shouldn't I?" she asked. "You did."

"But you're a better person than I ever was, darlin'. Everybody around here knows that."

In fact, he was exercising astounding restraint to keep from capitalizing on that kiss and seducing her right here and now. He knew the attraction was there on her part. He felt it every time he crushed her mouth beneath his. It was in her eyes when she looked at him. She wouldn't fight him. In fact, she would come to him as eagerly as she had at eighteen, when she'd been way too young and he'd been way too stupid to see what a gift she was giving him.

With the taste of her still on his lips, he made a hasty exit before he was tempted to stay and prove just how low-down and sneaky he could be.

Jo sank down on a kitchen chair after Pete had gone and touched a finger to her still burning lips. She could deny it from now till the cows came home, but she wanted him. It didn't seem to matter whether it was sensible or insane. It didn't seem to matter that he'd broken her heart once. All that mattered was the heat and need that simmered every time he was around. Even tinged with hurt and regret and anger, that need was a powerful force. In fact, its overwhelming power scared her to death. She liked being in control, but she wasn't with this. The need controlled her.

"You ought to be upstairs packing your bags right this second," she muttered aloud.

"Oh, my God," Maggie said, scaring Jo half to death. "She's in here talking to herself."

"Do you ever knock?" Jo groused as the door slammed shut behind all three sisters.

"Why would we?" Ashley asked reasonably. "We all have keys."

"Maybe you should turn them in to me. I'd like to know I can count on some privacy around here," Jo retorted.

"To do what?" Melanie asked, regarding her with amusement. "You having a fling you want to keep secret?"

There was no smart answer to that question, so Jo ignored it. A yes would definitely intrigue them. An honest answer—that she needed a break from them—would offend them.

"Why are you here?" she asked instead. "Just to make me nuts?"

"It's our sisterly duty to check on you," Ashley said.

"But daily? Is that really necessary?" she asked wryly.

"At a minimum," Ashley said. "Maybe more if we don't like what we find. Fortunately, it's a small town. It's not inconvenient for us to drop by."

Now *there* was a barely veiled threat, Jo concluded. She regarded her sisters with dismay. "Don't you all have husbands now?" she grumbled. "Shouldn't they be the focus of your attention?"

"You wish," Maggie said with a grin. "We know what they're up to. They're at my house grilling steaks. We give them an occasional men-only night, so they appreciate us more."

Jo laughed. "How's that working?"

"Amazingly well," Melanie complained. "We're beginning to think they get together just to talk about us and plot against us. It's worrisome."

"Really? Yet you still do it," Jo said with an exaggerated shake of her head. "Very sad. I thought you all were smarter than that. You were my role models. Now I'm not so sure I should pay a bit of attention to you *or* your unsolicited advice. What exactly do you think they're plotting?"

"Not so much plotting as exchanging information," Maggie said. "For instance, Rick came home the other night and insisted on fixing me dinner. He knows I'm the cook in the family. I take pride in it. But one of them must have told him it would be a treat for me to have a night off. He would never have thought of that on his own."

Jo stared at her. "Okay," she said slowly. "You say that as if it's a bad thing. What am I missing?"

Melanie nudged Maggie in the ribs. "Come on. Confess. You got all bent out of shape because you thought he was telling you he didn't like your cooking."

"Well, it did cross my mind," Maggie said, looking vaguely flustered by having to admit to an uncharacteristic dip in her normally healthy self-esteem in the kitchen. "But after my second glass of wine and my first taste of the pesto sauce he made from scratch, I decided maybe I should just go with the flow. The man seems to know his way around the kitchen. Who'd have guessed it?"

"And that's it?" Jo asked. "That's the kind of devious plotting they're up to over there tonight?"

"Pretty much," Ashley said.

"Well, thank God they haven't thought to include Pete yet," she said with exaggerated relief.

"Pete?" All three women seized on her comment at once.

"Should they be including Pete?" Ashley inquired,

her gaze narrowed. "What's happened? Do our men need to check him out more thoroughly? Should I run a check into his background? I can do that, no problem."

"Oh, stop it," Jo ordered. "Nothing's happened. I just meant that he *is* underfoot around here, so some people might leap to the conclusion that he should be dragged into this family mix thing. I was trying to make the point that I'm grateful he hasn't been lured into such a web of male intrigue."

"But these people who'd leap to that conclusion, they'd be wrong?" Ashley persisted. "You haven't done something crazy, have you?"

"Crazy like what?" Jo asked, struggling to contain her impatience.

"Well, you do want that stupid house," her big sister reminded her.

"We've been over this," Jo said irritably. "There are limits to what I'll do to get it."

"Glad to hear it," Ashley said. "I drove by it, by the way."

"Me, too," Melanie and Maggie chimed in.

"I can see why you adore it," Ashley said. "It's charming. It reminds me of Cape Cod."

Jo bit back a grin. "Maybe that's why they call that architecture the Cape Cod style."

Ashley frowned at her. "You're such a pain when you're being smug."

"If I'm so annoying, why didn't you all go to a movie tonight, instead of coming over here?"

"I think we've established that it's our duty to be here," Maggie said. "Whether you want us here or not. Let's play Scrabble. I'm feeling particularly brilliant tonight."

"Give her a glass of wine," Ashley ordered. "That ought to dull her brain. Nobody in this family is allowed to beat me at Scrabble."

"Is that so?" Jo asked, exchanging a look with her sisters. It was evident they were as eager as she to rise to the challenge. "What do you say, ladies? Do we make her regret those words?"

"I'm in," Melanie said at once.

"Oh, yes. I am so in," Maggie agreed.

Jo laughed. "Then, Maggie, you get the wine and I'll get the game. Just make sure you fill big sister's glass to the very brim. I'll have water, by the way."

"Me, too," Melanie said, winking at her.

Maggie nodded as she retrieved the glasses. "That'll be two waters and a brimming glass of wine for the smart-alecky big sister."

Ashley frowned at Maggie. "What about you? What are you drinking?"

Maggie plunked the wine bottle down at her own place at the table. "I'm going with the rest of the bottle."

"Oh, no," Melanie whispered, laughing. "That leaves me to drive them home and try to explain to Josh and Rick why they're drunk as skunks."

"I say we just pour them both into bed upstairs and let their husbands come and fetch them in the morning," Jo said. "Then we can watch while these two try to explain what happened. It'll be fun."

To her surprise, it was Ashley who regarded her with evident approval. "You have a very diabolical mind, little sister." She lifted her wineglass in a toast. "I salute you."

"Which should tell you something," Jo said.

"What?" Ashley asked, looking perplexed.

"That the rest of you can stop worrying about me. I'm not the nitwit you take me for. I can handle Pete Catlett and anything else that comes my way."

Her sisters exchanged a look, then grinned at her.

"You're our baby sister. We'll never stop worrying," Ashley said, patting her hand. "Get used to it."

Jo sighed. Right there in a nutshell was the primary reason she shouldn't even consider getting mixed up with Pete—or trying to buy that house that would keep her close to her overprotective sisters.

Somehow, though, as daunting as the prospect was, it wasn't nearly enough to stop the yearning for either one.

Chapter Nine

Fearing the confrontation that was bound to happen the minute he laid eyes on his ex-wife, Pete approached the ranch-style brick home he'd bought for Kelsey and his son with more than his usual trepidation. Kelsey's moods could be unpredictable at best. This morning, she might be humble and conciliatory, given the fact that she was clearly in the wrong, but more than likely she'd be defensive and spiteful.

This should have been such a tranquil place for Davey to grow up, Pete thought with another surge of anger. The house was in a quiet residential neighborhood with good schools nearby. It had cost more than he could afford at the time, but he'd wanted his son to have nothing but the best, and he'd been determined to be fair to Kelsey, too. Whatever else he thought of her, she would always be the mother of his son, and for that alone, he wanted to show her the respect she deserved.

Sometimes, though, she made it damn hard.

As he tried to settle his temper, he noticed that despite the money he sent her each month in alimony, none of it was apparently being spent on upkeep. The shutters needed painting and the garage door looked to be stuck halfway up.

He parked behind his ex-wife's brand-new SUV—a car which told him exactly where her money was going—and crossed the lawn to the front door. Davey came charging out before he got there and launched himself straight at Pete with a wild whoop of excitement.

"Hey, buddy," Pete said, laughing as he scooped the boy up and noted that his clothes were surprisingly neat for nine in the morning. Usually by now, Davey would have managed to make a mess of whatever he'd put on. "You look good." He buried his nose in the kid's stomach till Davey started giggling, then added, "Smell good, too."

"Mom let me take my bath this morning instead of last night, so I'd look good when you got here. Can I go next door and play now? Mom says you guys have gotta talk or something. Grown-up stuff, huh?"

"Yeah, it's grown-up stuff," Pete agreed. "I can't believe you want to play and spoil these nice, clean clothes." He paused, leaned closer, then asked with an expression of mock horror. "What if you have to take another bath?"

Davey giggled. "I'll be careful," he promised.

Pete rolled his eyes at the likelihood of that. "A half hour, pal. Then you and I are going to look for supplies for whatever it is you want to make as a science project."

"And we're having lunch out, too, right?"

"Absolutely. Whatever you want."

"Hamburgers and pizza," Davey said at once.

"That might be overdoing it," Pete said. "Think about it and pick one or the other. Now let me go in and say hello to your mom."

Davey was about to bound off down the street to his friend's house, but he suddenly turned and came back, his expression worried. "You and mom aren't gonna yell, are you?"

Pete tugged his son's baseball cap down over his eyes. "Nope."

"Promise?"

"I promise." It was a promise he had every intention of keeping, unless Kelsey failed to listen to reason.

Apparently satisfied, Davey took off running toward the neighbor's house. Pete watched till he went inside, then turned toward Kelsey's. When he walked in, he could hear the noise of cartoons coming from the family room and concluded that Davey had left the set on as usual. He listened some more and finally heard the faint sounds of water running in the kitchen. He headed in that direction.

Kelsey was at the kitchen sink, her hands in soapy dishwater. She stiffened when she heard him enter.

"Hey," Pete said, shrugging out of his jacket.

She turned slowly and he noted her unusually pale complexion and the worried expression on her face.

"I'm not going to jump down your throat again," he assured her.

She relaxed some at that. "Look, I'm sorry about what happened," she told him. "I honestly don't know what I was thinking. You were right. I was wrong."

He met her troubled gaze and reminded her, "You've said that before."

"I know, but we're living here in the land of families, and this place gets so damn lonely sometimes. I just wanted to go out with an adult for a change, instead of a carload of six-year-olds."

"Nothing wrong with that," Pete agreed, "but Davey can't be here by himself. Work out a deal with another mom to keep him, or find a reliable babysitter. I don't care what you do, but I meant what I said, Kelsey. If I find out he's here alone—and I don't care if you've just gone to the store for milk—I will go to court. I don't want to do that to him or to you, but I will. His safety is the priority here."

She looked thoroughly rattled by his quietly spoken declaration, more disconcerted than she might have been if he'd been shouting. "You really mean that, don't you?"

He nodded. "Yes."

She sucked in a deep breath and nodded. "Okay, then," she said. "I won't do anything to make you resort to that."

Pete prayed she'd keep that promise, but he knew from past history that the commitment could be just as fleeting as all her other promises. For now, though, he'd done all he could to warn her and to protect his son.

"So, how are you?" he asked. "Everything else okay?"

Her hands trembled slightly, but she nodded. "Great. What about you? Is everything good back home?"

"It's been busy," he told her. "I got several houses started and under roof this fall, so my crew's been working on the interiors now that the weather's a little rough out there."

"Anybody ask about me?" she inquired.

She sounded so wistful, Pete wished he honestly could say yes, but the truth was that most people in the town who knew both of them had taken his side in the divorce. They asked about Davey regularly, but any mention of Kelsey was likely to draw scowls, if not disdainful comments. Fortunately, they all knew better than to react that way when his son was around. He saw no point in telling her that, though.

"Sure," he said, choosing his words carefully. "You grew up there. Your name's bound to come up. People want to know how you're doing."

"What do you tell them?"

"That you're happy living in Richmond." He studied her intently. "You are happy, aren't you? This is what you wanted, after all."

Her cheeks flushed a bit at the reminder and for an instant he thought she might tell him the truth, for once, but then her pride apparently kicked in and she forced an obviously phoney smile. "I love it. Even here in 'Familyville,' it's better than that hick town any day."

"That's how I thought you felt," he said. "Though if you were ever to change your mind and decide you want to come home, we could get you a place down there. You know what it would mean to me to have Davey close by."

"Forget it," she said fiercely, either out of pride or some stubborn determination to keep him separated from his son. "You couldn't pay me enough to get me back there."

"Whatever," Pete said with a sigh. "Look, I'd better go next door and get Davey. Any particular time you want me to bring him back here?"

"Suit yourself," she said with unmistakable bitterness. "You're the one who insisted on coming today."

Pete told himself not to rise to the bait. "Then I guess I'll see you later. I'll have him back around five. I might stick around for an hour or so to help him with this science thing he's dreamed up."

His announcement was greeted with silence as Kelsey turned her back on him and went back to washing dishes. He stared at her with regret, then walked away.

Just once, he thought as he left the house, he wished that they could attain a level of civility and maintain it throughout his visit. It never failed, though, that something would set her off and the contact would turn, if not into an argument, then at least into a cold war of sorts.

It struck him then that his ex-wife was simply one of those people who would never be truly happy. She'd gotten exactly what she wanted with the divorce, custody of their son and this house in Richmond, but she still wasn't satisfied. It seemed likely she never would be, and that struck him as unbearably sad.

"So, can we, Dad?" Davey pleaded as Pete turned into the empty driveway at the house just before five o'clock.

Trying not to overreact to the obvious evidence that Kelsey had taken off, Pete forced his attention to his son. "Can we do what?"

"Weren't you listening?" Davey asked, his exasperation plain.

"Obviously not as well as I should have been," Pete told him, reaching over to muss up his hair. He'd lost his baseball cap somewhere along the way and his gloves. He probably would have left his jacket behind, too, but Pete had seen that on the floor under their table at the hamburger joint where they'd had lunch a few hours earlier. Pete had grabbed it before they left.

"I was asking if we could play a video game before you go home," Davey repeated.

"Sure, but what about that whole science thing you were so anxious to get into? We bought a whole bag full of stuff for that."

"Next time," Davey pleaded. "This game is so awesome. I want to show you."

"Okay, pal, a video game it is. Now grab that stuff from the backseat and I'll get the pizza." He'd bought a large one for dinner, thinking they would be sharing it with Kelsey.

They hadn't agreed to that, he reminded himself as he went inside. He couldn't get all worked up over her not being here. She was bound to be back soon. She knew he was bringing Davey back at five, because he'd told her.

But by the time he and Davey had eaten and played the video game for over an hour, there was still no sign of Kelsey. He sent his son off to take a bath and get ready for bed, then dialed Kelsey's cell phone number. She didn't pick up.

When Davey finally came padding downstairs, his hair standing up in damp spikes, his feet bare and his pajamas inside out, Pete had to bite back a grin. At least the kid had tried.

"Where's Mom?"

"I have no idea, buddy. She didn't leave a note."

Worry immediately creased his son's brow. "You're not going to go, are you?"

"No way. Come on. Let's go upstairs and I'll tuck you in. You can read me a bedtime story."

Davey giggled. "You're supposed to read it to me. I don't know enough words yet."

"Oh, that's right," Pete said. "I'd forgotten how it worked. You're so smart I figured you'd know a bunch of words by now. Maybe you could show me the ones you do know."

Davey nodded eagerly. "I could do that."

Upstairs, he picked a book from the stack beside his bed, then crawled in and scooted over to make room for Pete.

With his kid snuggled up next to him, Pete almost forgot about his exasperation with Kelsey. He'd missed nights like this. They were far too rare.

Together they read the story, but by the last page Davey's eyes were drifting shut. Pete closed the book, slipped off the bed, then pressed a kiss to Davey's forehead. "'Night, son."

Davey's blue eyes blinked open. "'Night, Dad. I love you."

"Back at you, kid."

After Davey drifted off again, Pete stood looking down at him, his heart filled with such aching joy he could hardly stand it. This boy was a part of him. He deserved nothing but the best, but he wasn't getting it, not from either of his parents. And there didn't seem to be a damn thing Pete could do to change that.

He went downstairs, poured himself a glass of milk, then settled into a chair in front of the TV to wait for his ex-wife.

His eyes repeatedly drifted closed, then snapped

open at some unexpected sound, but it was well after midnight when he finally heard Kelsey at the front door.

Pete flipped off the TV and stood up. When she rounded the corner into the family room, he stepped into her path. "Where the hell have you been?" he demanded, unable to keep his temper in check.

Defiance flashed in her eyes. "Out."

"Not good enough," he said coldly. "You knew I was bringing Davey back at five."

"You said you were going to stick around, so I figured there was no reason for me to be here, too," she said.

"An hour, Kelsey. I told you I'd be here an hour or so, not till after midnight. Dammit, didn't you hear anything I said to you earlier? Didn't your promise mean a damn thing?"

"Davey wasn't alone," she reminded him. "That was the deal."

He sighed at her twisted logic. "Is this the way it's going to be? Do you really want things to get complicated?"

She scowled at him. "Do whatever you need to do to feel like a big man, Pete. Frankly, I don't care."

He knew he'd pushed his luck by insisting on coming down here today, but he intended to push it even harder. It was past time he exerted a few more of his own parental rights, rather than bending over backward to keep things calm between them. Maybe she'd eventually get the message that he was losing patience with her games and that he was going to stick to the letter of the court's ruling, which guaranteed him a lot more time with Davey than he'd taken advantage of up till now for the sake of peace.

"Okay, then, this is what I need to do," he told her flatly. "I'll be back next Friday to pick Davey up from school. I'm taking him home with me for the long President's Day weekend."

Fear flashed in her eyes at that. "Oh, no, you're not. That's not one of his weekends to be with you. I didn't fight you this time, but I will fight you on that."

He regarded her with bemusement. "Why? It's obvious you'd rather be doing something besides taking care of our son. Consider this a bonus break for you. Besides, the court granted me four extended holiday visits a year. I intend to take this one."

"No."

"Why not?"

"Because you'll find some way to use it against me. I love that kid. You're not going to take him away from me. And I won't let you spend time turning him against me."

"You know I'd never do that, Kelsey," he responded patiently. "What's the real problem here?"

"I want him with me next weekend."

He knew better, but he asked anyway, "Did you already have something special planned?"

"No, but—"

Pete didn't know why he felt the need to push so hard for this, but he couldn't seem to let it go. He cut her off. "You need a break, Kelsey. Let me give it to you. I promise I won't hold it against you for saying yes to this. Have you ever known me to break my word?"

She looked as if she wanted to argue, but he knew she'd also started to consider what she could do with all that free time. "Okay, but just this once, right? You're not going to start making it a habit?"

"No. We'll stick to the schedule," he promised. To the letter, he added mentally.

"Okay, then. I'll let the school know you're coming on Friday."

They both knew it was a half-hearted attempt to prove she was in control. Both of their names were on the school list. Pete could have picked up his son without her permission, but he let her have her momentary feeling of power.

"Thanks. I'll call during the week to find out when you want him back on Monday, so there's no confusion."

She nodded, suddenly looked oddly defeated. "Look, it's late. Why don't you just stay till morning? You could see Davey again before you go."

Pete was tempted, but he'd learned a long time ago it was best not to accept Kelsey's hospitality. The last time he had, she'd tried to crawl into bed with him. Getting her out had been awkward and unpleasant.

"I'll be fine. I had a nap while I was waiting for you." He pulled on his jacket and headed from the room. When he turned back, she still looked so dejected that he came back and pressed a kiss to her forehead. "Take care of yourself."

"Yeah, sure," she murmured.

As he drove away, he realized she was standing in the shadows at the front window, staring after him. That, too, struck him as unbearably sad. It was the second time that day he'd felt a surge of pity for his ex-wife.

Pete was in an odd mood from the second he turned up on Monday morning. Once upon a time, Jo had been able to read him easily, but not this morning.

He'd arrived with another bag of those warm blueberry doughnuts, two extra large coffees and the usual lighthearted quips, but there was definitely something on his mind. There were unmistakable shadows in his eyes. To her dismay, she wanted to know what had put them there. She knew that asking would only draw her more deeply into his life, but she couldn't seem to stop herself from wondering.

Even as he was outside pounding nails into wood with more force than necessary, she watched him, startled by the anger and tension that seethed just beneath the surface. He hadn't said why he wasn't going on to another job site, and she hadn't asked about that, either. Maybe he was suddenly anxious to get this one finished so he could steer clear of her. She wasn't sure she wanted to know, if that was the case.

But by lunchtime, she'd had enough. Two could play at the game of poking and prodding.

"Lunch is ready," she announced cheerfully, enjoying the look of surprise in his eyes. He clearly hadn't been expecting the invitation. In fact, he didn't even look as if he'd realized what time it was.

Jo had made thick sandwiches with the leftover chicken, then made a pot of homemade vegetable soup with noodles, the way her grandmother used to make it. Pete eyed it suspiciously.

"You went to a lot of trouble."

"Hardly. It's soup and a sandwich, the same sort of thing you fixed me when you were worried about me."

"Does that mean you're worried about me?"

"Worried about all that lumber Ashley paid for, actually. The way you're pounding on it, I expect it to split."

"I know what I'm doing."

"I imagine you do," she agreed. "Usually, anyway. Otherwise I wouldn't see your name in front of half the houses under construction around here. Today must be some sort of off day."

"I don't want to talk about it," he said at once.

She studied him intently and concluded that the exact opposite was true. He was bursting to talk about whatever had him so upset.

"Is it that you don't want to get into it at all or that you don't think you should get into it with *me?*"

His expression turned sad. "There was a time we could talk about anything," he said, a wistful note in his voice.

She nodded. "We still can, even if it has something to do with your marriage or your son. Is that it? Didn't things go well when you went to see him?"

He gave her a hard, searching look. "Are you sure you won't mind if I get into this?"

"I won't know until you start, will I?"

He told her about his call from his son and then his argument with his ex-wife. Before he could go on, Jo was already seething with indignation. "She actually left a six-year-old boy by himself at night?" she demanded incredulously. "How could she do something so irresponsible?"

"Then I'm not crazy?" he said, looking oddly relieved by her immediate and forceful reaction. "That is a really lousy idea?"

"Well, of course, it is. What was she thinking?"

"She wasn't thinking. She was on a date and she was drinking. It happens more than it should. In fact, it might have happened again night before last, but I was there. I stuck around till she finally wandered in after midnight."

"Then you have to do something," Jo said flatly. "Protecting your son is the only thing that matters."

Oddly, talking about Pete's son didn't hurt half as much as she'd expected it to. In fact, she found herself longing for a glimpse of him. She already knew from his picture that he looked just like his dad, but what about his personality? Was he full of mischief? Was he smart as a whip, the way Pete had been?

"I wish I could meet Davey," she said, then faltered. "But that's probably a bad idea."

"Why would it be?" he asked. "At least from my perspective. What about you, though? Are you sure you really want to see him? I would certainly understand if you never wanted to set eyes on him."

"How can you say that? What happened wasn't his fault. And he's a part of you. Of course I'd love to meet him."

"Then you can have your chance to do that next weekend," he announced, catching her by surprise. "I'm picking Davey up on Friday. He'll be here till Monday. If you're sure about this, we could get together on Saturday and do something."

A part of her wanted to agree, wanted to say, "Of course, bring him by." But somewhere deep inside, she was terrified of what might happen next. What if she fell in love with Pete's little boy? He would never be hers. In fact, he was likely to be snatched away from her. Could she bear that? And how would his mother feel about Pete introducing another woman into Davey's life—especially *her?* Would it only cause more problems between Pete and his ex?

In the end, though, it was the prospect of yet more heartache for herself that led her to a decision.

"I'm sorry," she whispered eventually, "I think maybe it's a bad idea, after all."

She would have run from the room so Pete couldn't see the tears gathering in her eyes, but he stopped her before she could take the first desperate step.

"I'm the one who's sorry," he said, gathering her close. "For everything. I shouldn't have asked."

She managed a watery smile. "It was my idea," she reminded him. "Then I got scared."

"Of what?"

"Falling for a six-year-old and then losing him the way I did his dad."

Pete closed his eyes and pulled her close again. She could feel the steady beat of his heart under her cheek. It was reassuring and familiar.

"Just think about it," he said at last. "I swear I won't push you, but he's such a great kid. I'd like you to know him. And I'd like him to meet you."

"How will you explain who I am? Or has he met a lot of women in your life?"

"There haven't been a lot of women in my life since his mom and I split up, but Davey hasn't met any of them. You'd be the first."

Her heart flipped over at that. "Then why me?" she asked.

His gaze locked with hers. "Don't you know?"

She was afraid to guess. "No."

"Because you matter, Jo. You always have."

Chapter Ten

Jo's head was spinning. She'd never expected Pete to tell her that she mattered to him, not like that, not so soon. She'd almost come unglued and burst into tears right there in his arms. Wouldn't that have been a pretty picture?

She couldn't let those impulsively spoken words turn her world topsy-turvy, she told herself a thousand times in the following days. It wasn't as if he'd declared his undying love, after all. *You matter to me,* that's what he'd said. Not *I love you.* Heck, the accountant who kept his company books probably *mattered* to him. So did the guys on his crew.

But even though she tried hard to put those four simple words in perspective, Jo kept hearing the underlying meaning in his voice. It was as close to an admission of love as he could give her right now, probably as close as he thought she could accept.

But was it enough to give her the strength it would take to meet his little boy? That child, through no fault of his own, had changed her life forever. How would she react when she saw him? She knew instinctively that she would open her heart to him, and that terrified her most of all.

But as terrified as she was of being hurt again, Jo knew she had no real choice. She wanted to see that child, to get to know him, to see how much of Pete she would find in his eyes. If anguish and regrets over dreams lost came with that, so be it. That was a small enough price to pay for sharing something—someone— so important to Pete.

Even though her decision was essentially made, she kept it to herself. She didn't want to have to take her words back later if she chickened out. She could tell, though, that her silence on the subject was driving Pete just a little bit crazy. He'd promised not to push her, so he wouldn't, but every time they were together during the week, he watched her, his gaze questioning, asking all the questions he'd promised not to verbalize.

Finally, on Thursday, Jo couldn't stand the wary, sur-reptitious glances another second.

"Okay, yes," she said as they drank coffee and ate doughnuts at the kitchen table in what was turning into their morning ritual. It felt so damn comfortable and right, that the routine scared her, too.

Pete blinked and stared at her. "Yes?"

"Let's all do something together on Saturday. You, me and Davey."

His eyes lit up and a smile spread across his face. It was as if she'd granted his wish or something. Perhaps if she'd realized how much it meant to him, she would have told him sooner.

"Really?" he asked. "You're sure?"

She held up a cautioning hand. "Let's not make a big commotion out of it, though, okay?"

His gaze narrowed. "Meaning?"

"We could just hook up at one of the sites, make it look accidental. You know, like it's no big deal."

He looked as if he might argue, but evidently he, too, saw the wisdom in that. "You're probably right," he said at last. "That would be best."

"Then, if you wanted, we could grab some lunch or something. Maybe a burger. Does he like hamburgers?"

"Next to pizza, they're his favorite."

"Would it be better to go for pizza, then?" she asked worriedly, wanting this meeting to go right. She knew she was placing way too much importance on it, but she couldn't seem to help herself. No matter how they played it, for her it would be a very big deal.

Pete reached across the table and put his hand on hers. "Hey, stop fussing. We're not going to place too much importance on this, remember?"

"I know, I know. I don't want to make a big production out of it for your son's sake, but for me it's different." She drew in a deep breath and steadied her resolve. "That doesn't mean it needs to be a big deal for him, though. I just want him to have a good time, do things he enjoys doing, you know?"

"You want him to like you," Pete concluded, cutting straight through to the bottom line.

"Okay, yes," she admitted, chagrined.

Pete grinned at her. "With any luck, all of this plotting every minute will be wasted, anyway."

"Why?" she asked in alarm, fearing that her already out-of-control hopes were about to be dashed. "Do you think he might not come?"

"Oh, he's coming," Pete said, his expression filled with grim determination. "But there's snow in the forecast for Friday night. Quite possibly, we'll be able to spend Saturday sledding and building snowmen." He winked at her. "Then I can send the kid to bed and you and I can get all cozy in front of a fire."

The prospect sounded so inviting, she forced herself to put up at least a token protest. "I don't think so."

"Why not?"

"With your son in the house?" she asked, her tone chiding.

He gave her a piercing look, as if he'd read something into the comment she hadn't intended. "What about after he goes home?" he asked. "Can we get cozy then?"

She met his gaze and made a decision that had been a long time coming, even though it had been inevitable. "I'd have to say that's a definite maybe."

"Not as much conviction as I'd like to hear, but I'll take it as a positive sign," he said. "Now I can hardly wait to take the kid home. What kind of father does that make me?"

"A human one," she said. "And maybe it's something you need to remember when your ex-wife doesn't stop to think. She's only human, too."

"The difference is that I would never leave Davey on

his own, no matter how desperate I was to be with someone else."

Jo slid out of her chair and walked around to the
other side of the table. Impulsively, she slipped onto
Pete's lap and cupped his face in her hands. "I know.
That's what makes you amazing."

Heat immediately blazed in his eyes. "And I thought
all along it was my hard muscles you liked."

"Nope. Your tender heart," she told him, tapping on
his chest.

"You know," he said quietly, "Davey's not here now."

She met his gaze, her heart in her throat. "I know, but
there's no snow on the ground, either."

"Do you think that's entirely necessary?"

Her heart tumbled to her toes as an old and wonder-
fully familiar desire nearly overwhelmed her. "Now that
you mention it, I don't think it's necessary at all."

In the back of his mind, Pete had been imagining this
moment for days now, maybe even weeks. Maybe forever. Now that it was here, he could hardly believe it was
real. He stroked a finger along Jo's cheek just to reas-
sure himself it wasn't a dream.

"Nope," he murmured. "Definitely real."

"Make love to me," she said, her hand on his cheek.
"That ought to convince you I'm very real."

He knew he should keep his questions to himself
and accept this precious gift, but he couldn't seem to
stop himself from asking, "Why now?"

Her lips curved. "Why not now? Are you going to
talk this to death? I thought men were the impulsive,
spontaneous ones when it came to sex."

Pete knew he had to be candid with her. As desperately as he wanted this, he didn't want to make a mistake they'd both regret. "It's been a very long time, Jo. A lot's happened between us. If I take you upstairs now, if I make love to you, it's not going to be the start of some casual fling. It's going to mean something."

She swallowed hard. "Please don't say that," she said, her gaze pleading.

"I have to say it. You need to understand where my head is. I'm not saying you have to be in the same place, but you need to know how I feel." He looked into her eyes. "I guess, in a way, I'm giving you the power to hurt me, because I'm telling you that my heart's on the line. You'll be able to get even with me for what I did," he said. "Or you can love me back."

To his dismay, a tear spilled down her cheek. "Dammit, Pete. Don't you know how I feel? I *do* love you. I don't want to, but I do."

He chuckled despite her obvious distress. "Now there's a declaration guaranteed to make a man's heart sing."

She nudged him in the stomach with her elbow. "Don't joke about this."

"I know, darlin'. It's not a laughing matter."

"No, it's not."

He looked into her eyes. "Does that mean we're not messing around?"

Her lips twitched, then broke into a wide smile, the kind of smile that had once twisted his heart into knots.

"Think you can beat me up those stairs?" she taunted, already out of his lap and heading for the doorway.

Laughing, Pete caught up with her in two strides and

scooped her into his arms. "How about we get there to-gether?" he said as he took the stairs two at a time.

"I think I'm beginning to admire those muscles more than I did before," she said as he carried her without hesitation into the right bedroom. "How'd you know which room I'd be in?"

"I stood outside under your window often enough when I was a lovesick twenty-year-old. I know which room is yours." He glanced around. "I've just never had a chance to see it from the inside before."

It was a girly room with lots of pale pink and soft green in the flowery materials of the comforter on the old iron bed. The bed was piled with lace-trimmed pillows. There was a dark burgundy stripe in the cream wallpaper that somehow tied it all together and made it just right for the sexy woman she'd become.

He sat down on the edge of the bed and pulled her into the *V* between his thighs. Holding her loosely, he gave the mattress a test bounce, then grinned. "Good. No squeaks."

"Even if there were, there's no one in the house to hear them," she said. "Do you realize we've never actually made love in a bed before?"

Pete frowned at that. It was true. They'd had to steal their moments to be together and be inventive about their privacy. He pulled her closer. "Then I think it's way past time to change that, don't you?"

"I don't know," she said. "I thought there was something awfully exciting and special about trying not to get caught."

"Ah, so it was the thrill that got to you back then," he teased. "It had nothing to do with me. In that case, let me run downstairs, unlock the front door and make a call to your sisters. Knowing they could turn up at any second could add a little spice to the afternoon."

"Heaven forbid," Jo said fervently. "They can't know about this."

Pete's heart thumped unsteadily at the implication. "Why not?"

"For your protection," she said at once.

"My protection?" he echoed, stunned. "Why on earth do you need to protect me?"

She grinned at him. "Let's think about this. We're talking about three overly protective big sisters, who've just recently gone from whirlwind courtships into marriage. Can you connect the dots yet?"

Pete saw her point, but he wasn't nearly as terrified by the outcome as she apparently was. "Think they'll try to push us into walking down the aisle?"

"I know they will," she confirmed.

"Maybe that's not such a bad thing. It's what should have happened seven years ago," he said.

"No," she said fiercely. "That was clearly the wrong time for us. Either you would never have had your son or he would have been born without a father. Can you honestly say either of those would have been for the best?"

"No," he admitted. As much as he regretted the way things had turned out for him and Jo, he could never regret having Davey. He tunneled his fingers into her hair and looked deep into her eyes. "Do you have any idea how amazingly generous you are?"

"Me?"

"Yes, you. You're thoughtful and smart and sexy, too."

"All those things?" she said, clearly pleased. "I *am* amazing. Maybe I'm too good for the likes of you."

"You are," he said at once. "Which makes me the luckiest man on the face of the earth since you're here with me now."

Jo lowered her face until her lips were almost on his. "Then let's take advantage of your luck," she whispered right before her mouth settled against his.

Pete felt his pulse jolt, then scramble. His blood shot straight from his brain to another part of his anatomy. He still had just enough sense left to remind himself to go slow, to savor this moment, to savor *her.*

He took that soft, sweet kiss and turned it into something greedy and primal. Jo turned restless, her body seeking his, rubbing against hardness and heat and need in a way that almost had him bolting off the bed.

"Slow down, darlin'," he whispered against her fantastically seductive mouth.

In response, she took his hand and slid it up under her sweater until it met flesh and lace. She was so hot, so soft, Pete wanted to bury his face between her breasts, wanted to stroke his tongue over the hard, sensitive peaks until she was moaning with pleasure.

But not just yet, he told himself. He wouldn't rush her or himself. He'd waited seven years for this. He could wait a little longer, make sure that she knew what a treasure she was, what pleasure she was capable of giving and receiving. He'd been too impatient at twenty. He'd loved her then, but not well—not with a man's patience and desire.

He did, however, strip away that soft sweater so he could gaze at her full breasts and the surprising black lace bra that was such a contrast to the innocence of the plain white garment she'd worn all those years ago. Sexy as this was, he almost regretted the change, or maybe what he really regretted was the loss of innocence. It was something he'd taken and could never give back.

He skimmed a finger across the lace, smiled as she trembled. "Fancy," he said, grinning.

"When I turned twenty-one, my sisters thought it was time to upgrade my lingerie wardrobe." She winked at him. "Wait till you see the pitiful excuse for panties I'm wearing."

Pete moaned. "Don't tell me that. I'm trying to cling to some control here."

"Why?"

"Because you deserve to be properly seduced."

"And you can't do that if I start talking about my skimpy little lace thong?"

He covered his ears. "No, I cannot."

"It's black, too."

Pete groaned.

She grinned. "Good to know just how to rattle you," she said, reaching for the zipper on her jeans and slowly sliding it down.

Pete tried not to look, because he knew he'd be lost. Slow and sweet would be out of the question if those panties were half as sexy as she'd implied.

One glimpse of black lace and he nearly swallowed his tongue. There was barely enough there to cover…well, anything. He finally tore his gaze away and met her eyes.

"I warned you," he whispered, scooping her up and

settling her on the bed. He reached for her jeans and yanked them down and off with one smooth motion, then turned all his attention to that skimpy little bit of fabric.

He cupped her, rubbing fabric against the sensitive bud that was already hard, then slipped two fingers over flesh and deep into moist heat. She convulsed around him, her hips lifting off the bed. A ragged moan tore from her throat.

That was all it took to strip away his last shred of control. He kicked off his own jeans and Jockey shorts, then ripped those dangerously wicked little pants right off of her before plunging into her with a thrust that had her bucking against him.

He stayed perfectly still, counting to ten, thinking about the weather, doing anything he could not to give in to the desire to claim her for his own once and for all time. She whimpered against his throat and her hips moved with a will of their own, seeking, pleading, demanding.

Pete looked into her eyes and saw the yearning, the hunger that he knew was reflected in his own and then he began to move, faster and then faster still until the heat and tension exploded, sending shudders rocking through both of them.

It was a long, long time before his brain cleared enough to think, before he could shift his weight off of her to roll over, carrying her with him. He caught a finger through the ruined scrap of lace and dangled it in the air. "I'll buy you a dozen more just like this," he promised.

"Oh, sweet heaven," she murmured, her breath still ragged. "Forget the panties. What have you done to me? I'm limp."

Pete grinned and shifted beneath her. "I'm not."

She gave him a startled look and then a smile spread across her face. "No, indeed. You're definitely not. I suppose it's up to me to do something about that."

He laughed. "Only if you feel so inclined," he said, putting his hands behind his head and waiting.

She rose up and settled herself astride him. He watched her face as she rode him, laughed at her exultant expression, but then his body went on a wild ride of its own. His vision blurred, his breath snagged in his chest and for just a minute, he was pretty sure he could reach out and touch heaven.

Jo woke to the sound of a door closing downstairs. She rolled over, expecting to find nothing but empty mattress, but there was Pete, still beside her, still looking magnificent and very, very naked.

Which meant that door downstairs had been opened and closed by one of her sisters…or all three of them. She bolted out of bed as if someone had lit a fire under her. She peeked out the window, praying that she would see them driving away, probably confused by not finding her inside, but none the wiser about how she'd spent her day.

But, no, there was Maggie's car—right behind Pete's pickup—and not a sign of Maggie herself, which meant Jo's goose was cooked. Probably well done, in fact.

She frantically pulled on clothes without stopping to consider the effect, then shook Pete. He blinked sleepily and reached for her.

"Not now," she whispered, pushing his hands away.

"Sister alert. I'm going downstairs. Whatever you do, do not follow me. Understand?"

He gave her a vague smile and rolled over, burying his face in the pillow. She rolled her eyes and headed for the door, then thought about it and took the time to run a brush through her tangled hair. There wasn't much she could do about her swollen lips, except to touch them up with fresh lipstick.

Five minutes later, she walked into the kitchen, yawning mightily. Three expectant faces turned to her.

"Hey, you guys. I didn't know you were here. Why didn't you wake me?"

"We just got here," Melanie said, then tried ineffectively to swallow a chuckle.

Ashley didn't seem nearly as amused. "I hope, just in the nick of time," she said.

"Oh, please," Maggie chimed in, not even attempting to hide her own amusement. "Nick of time? Not unless Jo's wardrobe has taken a serious dive into flannel."

Jo glanced down and realized for the first time that the shirt she'd grabbed was Pete's. It hung down to her knees and was buttoned so haphazardly, there was no mistaking the haste with which she'd put it on.

"Oh, no," she whispered and sank onto a chair. "I wanted so much to pull this off."

"What?" Ashley inquired. "A deception? You wanted to lie to us?"

Jo's chin rose a notch. "Yes, as a matter of fact."

Her oldest sister looked stunned. "But why?"

"Because you're going to get all protective and nosy and pushy. I know you, remember?"

"We love you. We're concerned," Ashley said. "You should appreciate that."

"And I do, in a general, nonspecific sort of way. But right here and now, with you three in my face, I could live without it."

"I just have one question for you," Ashley said. "What kind of man would let you come down here alone to face us?"

"A man who was instructed to stay put," Jo said.

"In your bed, I presume," Ashley said.

"Yes, in my bed. I'm a grown woman. I get to decide who's in my bed."

"And you want Pete Catlett there?" her sister persisted.

"Yes," Jo said emphatically.

"And it has nothing to do with that house you want?" Ashley pressed.

Jo scowled at her. "Do you have any idea how insulting it is that you would even ask me that?"

"It is," Melanie and Maggie agreed.

Ashley didn't look fazed by their reaction. "It's a fair question. Why is that man in your bed?"

"Because I love him, dammit!" she all but shouted. "There, are you satisfied?"

Filled with heat and dismay and anger, she grabbed her jacket off a hook by the door and slammed out of the house. At first, the frigid blast of air felt good against her overheated flesh, but within seconds she knew it was too darn cold to be going for a walk just to get away from her sisters. Worse, she hadn't brought her keys, so she couldn't even go and sit in the car with the heater on. Then she thought of Pete's truck out front and the keys he usually left in the ignition.

"Thank you," she muttered gratefully with a glance toward her bedroom window. She climbed into the pickup and started the engine. In no time, the heater kicked in and the windows steamed up.

When the passenger door opened, she didn't even turn. "Go away. I'm not talking to you."

It was Pete who responded. "Not even to me?" he asked quietly.

Jo sighed. "I probably shouldn't be talking to you, either, but no, you're not the problem. Well, you are, but not the one that has me ticked off at the moment."

He studied her for what seemed like an eternity, then chuckled. "I like the way that flannel looks on you. I'll never be able to wear that shirt again without getting turned on."

"Don't even mention this blasted shirt to me," she grumbled. "I might have pulled this off if I hadn't grabbed it by mistake."

"Maybe it wasn't a mistake," he said. "Maybe you wanted them to know."

She frowned at him. "Believe me, I did not want them to know about us."

"Are you so sure? Maybe you were hoping they'd kick up such a fuss it would give you an excuse to call things off before they get any more complicated."

"No," she said with certainty. "I wanted time, Pete."

"Time for what?"

"To figure out if we can get it right this time."

"Oh, darlin'," he whispered, pulling her into his arms. "We've got all the time in the world for that."

"Did you see those three?"

"Actually, no. I did the cowardly thing and snuck out

the front door after I saw you crawl into my truck. When I heard the engine turn over, I was afraid you might just head for Montana to get away from all those prying eyes."

"Definitely not a bad idea. They're sitting in there waiting to pounce all over this. It's Ashley mostly, but even Maggie and Melanie will get in on the act sooner or later."

"Then tell them to butt out."

"I did," she said.

"And then you ran out here to hide in my truck. You let them chase you out of your own house."

She regarded him with dismay. "I did, didn't I? I gave them all the power. How stupid was that?" She cut the engine and wrenched open the door, but before she could climb out of the truck, Pete pulled her back.

"Hold on," he said.

"I need to go back in there and tell them to butt out."

He grinned. "In a minute."

She stared at him blankly. "Why wait?"

"For this," he said, and kissed her till her head went spinning. He grinned, obviously satisfied. "Now, then, warrior princess, let's go get 'em."

"You don't need to get involved," she protested. "You could leave."

"I am involved." His grin spread. "Besides, I can't very well leave without my shirt, and I doubt you want to strip it off and give it to me before you go back inside. Neither one of us would hear the end of that."

Jo laughed at the image of her sisters' reaction to that. "Might be worth it," she said. "Then again, it might be smarter to go in there with backup."

He winked at her. "Always said you were smart."

Jo suddenly felt stronger, as if she really could conquer the world. Then, again, she'd settle for keeping her sisters' noses out of her business.

Chapter Eleven

Pete had to admire the way Jo stood up to her sisters, all but daring them to make a comment when they came in from the truck with him wearing his undershirt and jacket and Jo still in his flannel shirt. She stared them down when all three women gave him smiles that made his blood run cold. The tactic was only partially success-ful. They pretty much ignored her and kept their focus on him.

"Hello, Pete," Ashley said, her voice frosty.

"Hey, Ashley. Good to see you."

"Do you know Maggie and Melanie?"

He nodded at them, feigning total composure. "Nice to meet you," he said, even as he thought that only an idiot wouldn't recognize this polite charade for what it was—the prelude to an inquisition.

"We've heard a lot about you," Melanie said, barely containing a grin.

"But apparently not nearly as much as we should have," Ashley said, casting a pointed look in Jo's direction.

There went the gloves, Pete thought, and waited to see how Jo reacted. Adding to his deep respect for her, Jo beamed at Ashley.

"I thought you knew all you needed to," she informed her older sister. "You're the one who hired Pete, right? And he had worked for you before. I figured you'd checked him out six ways from Sunday before you called him the first time."

Ashley frowned at the retort. "Actually, Josh was the one who found him to do the work for us. I trusted my husband's judgment."

"Well, there you go," Jo said triumphantly. "And Pete must have done good work, or you'd never have called him to do another job for you, correct?"

"I called him to fix the porch," Ashley said impatiently. "Not to sleep with you. You have to admit the qualifications are somewhat different."

"Then I guess it's just a lucky bonus for me that's he more than qualified to do both," Jo said gaily, while Pete choked back a laugh. "Now if you all don't mind, Pete and I have things to do this afternoon."

Ashley looked absolutely stunned. "You're kicking us out?"

"Pretty much," Jo said without hesitation.

Pete regarded her with admiration. He gave her a thumbs-up signal that put a smile back on her lips.

"Next time you might want to call first," she told her sisters. "Make sure I'm not going to be busy before you drop in. Perhaps we'll be able to avoid another of these awkward situations."

"You've changed," Ashley told her. "I'm not sure I like it." She frowned at Pete. "Is this your doing?"

"You mean Jo standing up for herself?"

"Is that what you call it?" Ashley asked.

"Sounds that way to me. And no, it's not my doing. I think she's always had it in her."

Ashley's gaze instantly narrowed, and Pete realized he'd gone too far.

"Now how would you know that?" Ashley asked him.

Pete read the panic in Jo's eyes and knew he had to extricate himself from the inadvertent slip. "Don't you think most people are born with a certain amount of strength? They just have to learn how to tap into it."

Relief shone in Jo's eyes.

Ashley still looked skeptical, but she didn't force his hand. Instead, she turned to her sisters. "Are you guys ready to go? We're obviously in the way here."

"Personally I think it's a lot more fascinating here," Maggie said, but she got to her feet. Melanie followed.

After a flurry of goodbyes, they were gone. Jo sagged onto the chair next to Pete.

"Oh, my God," she murmured.

"You were great!"

She whirled on him. "Great? Are you crazy? Thanks to that expression of insolence and ingratitude, I have just launched a full-scale investigation into our private lives that won't end till we've walked down the aisle of some church. They left quietly enough, but only so they can go someplace and plan some scheme that will hit us when we least expect it. Just wait till they get their husbands in on it. Our lives won't be worth living. We'll never have another second's peace."

"But we're on to them," Pete reminded her, unfazed by her panic. "They won't catch us off guard. Besides, what can they do, really?"

"Make our lives a living hell?" she suggested, her tone deadly serious.

"Come on. It won't be that bad."

"Ha!"

"Want to go back upstairs so I can show you why it's all going to be worthwhile?"

She shot him a withering look. "That's what got us into this mess."

He shook his head. "No, what got us into this was the fact that we couldn't keep our hands to ourselves. We never could. Personally, I think that speaks volumes."

"No, that should have been a lesson to us seven years ago," she retorted. "You'd think we'd be smarter now."

"We are," he insisted. "We're smart enough to go after what we want and fight for it. I want you. What do you want?"

"The truth?"

"Of course."

"The only thing I know with absolute certainty that I want is that house."

Pete's heart sank. He knew this afternoon hadn't been about the house, but he never in his life would have guessed he could be jealous of a pile of shingles and some hardwood floors.

He forced himself to respond with a careless shrug. "Maybe one of these days you'll decide to take the package deal."

In fact, he was counting on it.

* * *

Jo's thoughts were such a jumble, she didn't know which problem to grapple with first. She was going to have to deal with her sisters sooner or later. She wasn't naive enough to believe that kicking them out of Rose Cottage had been anything more than a temporary reprieve. She was going to have to figure out what to do about her feelings for Pete, which were getting more powerful and more complicated by the day. And she was going to have to spend time with his son without letting her heart get broken.

So many problems and not a solution in sight, she thought wearily.

Fortunately, for one day at least, she could simply avoid the whole lot of them. She was up and out of the house before daybreak on Friday. She merely got in her car and set out on an aimless drive. At least that was how it started.

She realized once she'd stopped for breakfast and caffeine that what she was really on was a research mission. She wanted to study the landscaping around the region, see what plants were thriving, which ones didn't seem to do well, and which created the old-fashioned country cottage or beach house ambience she wanted at both of Pete's houses. It would be better to do this sort of tour in spring or summer, but midwinter was the only time she had to do it. She'd just have to use her expertise and imagination to fill in the gaping blanks.

Since she'd been in the habit of doing this sort of thing whenever she went for a drive back in Boston, she had a pad and pencil handy in the car so she could jot down notes every time she stopped by the side of the road. By the time she got back to Rose Cottage at dusk, the pad was filled with scribbled notes and sketches. At least one thing in her life was under control, she thought happily right before she spotted Ashley's car in the driveway. If only the rest were, she added with a sigh.

She emerged from her own car reluctantly and went inside. She found her sister sitting in the kitchen with a cup of tea and a troubled expression.

"Where have you been?" Ashley asked. "With Pete, I assume, since he's nowhere to be found, either."

"Actually I've been working," Jo said, tossing the pad of paper on the table. "Doing some research. And I was alone, not that it's any of your business."

The sketches and notes distracted Ashley for a time. She turned the pages slowly, grinning from time to time.

"These are good. Really good," she told Jo.

"Thanks, but I'm sure you didn't come by to tell me I'm good at my job."

"No, To be honest, I came by to tell you to watch yourself with Pete."

"You're the one who sent him over here," Jo reminded her again. "If you meant him to be nothing more than eye candy, you should have said as much at the beginning. Maybe plastered a look-but-don't-touch sign on his very attractive behind."

Ashley didn't seem to appreciate the humor. "I know. I did think he'd provide a good distraction, get your mind off the broken engagement." She regarded Jo worriedly. "I might have made a mistake."

"Hold the presses!" Jo exclaimed. "You're admitting to a mistake?"

"It's not a joke," Ashley said. "I'm trying to tell you

something here. Pete's life is a mess. I didn't realize that. He has an ex-wife and a son."

"I know."

Ashley looked surprised. "He told you, then? That's something, I suppose."

"Did you really think he'd try to hide it? It's a small town. I was bound to find out." She wasn't about to admit that she'd known about the marriage and the son for years.

"I wasn't sure. I don't know him that well. I gather the divorce wasn't pretty. There's probably a lot of baggage there. You've already been through a lot, Jo. Why go looking for more trouble?"

"I appreciate your concern. I really do. But you don't need to worry. I'm on full alert where Pete's concerned." If only Ashley knew just how alert, she might take some comfort in it. Then, again, it might only make her worry more.

Ashley studied her somberly, then finally gave her a satisfied nod. "Okay, then. I'll butt out."

Jo grinned. "As if you could."

"I'll *try* to butt out," Ashley amended.

Jo crossed the room and hugged her fiercely. "Thanks. Now go home to your husband."

"What are you going to do tonight? Want to come to dinner?"

"No, I think I'll stay here. I have a lot going on right now."

"Pete coming by?" Ashley inquired with feigned nonchalance.

"Less than a minute and she's butting back in again," Jo teased. "No, Pete is not coming by. He's in

Richmond picking up his son. Davey's coming for the weekend."

"Oh, I see." Ashley studied her intently. "How do you feel about that?"

"Ask me after tomorrow."

"Why then?"

"I'm going to spend the day with them. I'll be able to give you a better answer."

Ashley gave her shoulder a squeeze. "I almost wish you hadn't told me that. Now I'll be worried sick all day. Do you think it's a good idea for you to spend time with his son? Not just for your sake, but for the boy's?"

"See what happens when you go poking around for information?" Jo teased. "Sometimes you find out things you'd rather not know. And believe me, Pete and I have discussed all the pitfalls. We're going to make sure it doesn't turn into a big deal."

Once more, her sister frowned at her joking. "Promise me one thing."

"Anything."

"Don't get your heart broken."

Jo nodded. "That one's easy. I'm certainly going to try like hell not to."

She was just terrified it might be easier said than done.

Pete was jostled awake at dawn on Saturday when Davey started bouncing on his bed, his face alight with excitement.

"Guess what, Dad?" He nudged Pete. "Are you awake?"

"How could I not be awake? Somebody's using my

bed for a trampoline," Pete mumbled sleepily. "What's up, buddy? Couldn't you sleep?"

Davey gave him a disgusted look. "I slept, but then morning came, and I got up," he explained with exaggerated patience. "Come on, Dad. You still haven't guessed."

Pete was pretty sure he knew based on the way his son's eyes were shining, but he pretended to give the question serious thought. "I know," he said at last. "The tooth fairy came and left a million dollars under your pillow."

Davey giggled. "No." He opened his mouth wide. "See. All my teeth are still there." He wiggled one in front. "This one's getting ready to go, though. Will I get a million dollars?"

"Not likely, kid. So, if it's not that, what could it be?"

"It snowed!" Davey said, obviously thrilled. "And not just a little bit, either. Lots and lots! Can we go outside?"

Pete glanced at the clock. It was barely 6:30. "How about breakfast first? Maybe by the time we're done, it will at least be daylight."

"But I want to build a snow fort."

"And you don't think you'll have time to do that if we start at, say, seven-thirty?"

"But that's a whole hour from now," Davey protested.

"Trust me, the time will fly by. It takes a long time to make pancakes and eat them."

The mention of pancakes immediately wiped the beginnings of a pout off of his son's face. "Big ones or little ones?"

"Does it matter?"

"I like the little ones," Davey announced.

"Any particular reason?"

"Sure. 'Cause then I can eat about a hundred of them."

Pete rolled his eyes. "In that case, you'd better go in the kitchen and check to see if we've got enough pancake mix. You can get it out of the cabinet and find a big bowl, but do not, I repeat, do not, get started till I get in there."

"But I can pour the flour into the bowl," Davey said.

And onto the table and the floor, Pete imagined. "Wait for me," he repeated firmly. "Ten minutes, okay?"

"Okay," Davey agreed and ran out of the room at full throttle.

Pete grinned. Oh, to have that much energy again. He rolled over, picked up the phone and called Jo. She answered groggily.

"Did you know it snowed last night?" he asked.

"Is this one of those nuisance calls?" she grumbled. "I'm hanging up."

"You'll be sorry," he said. "And no, it's not a nuisance call. It's a news alert. Snow means the plans have changed."

"Changed how?"

"We need to get started a whole lot earlier, because little boys can hardly wait to get outside."

She laughed. "How about big boys?"

"Personally, I could have used another hour of sleep, but I'm not the one who counts over here. Get moving, darlin'. We'll meet you at your favorite house at eight-thirty, unless you want to switch gears and come over here for pancakes."

She was silent so long, Pete knew she was wrestling with the choice, but eventually she sighed.

"Let's stick to the plan," she said with an unmistakable hint of regret in her voice. "I'll see you at eight-thirty. Are we building a snowman or sledding?"

"We're building a snow fort. And just so you know, forts take time when they're crafted by Catlett Construction. Wear something warm."

"You're talking to a woman from Boston. We know how to dress for snow. See you soon."

Pete was smiling as he hung up, but a glance at the clock showed him he needed to hurry. Davey wouldn't wait forever for those pancakes. He'd either turn the kitchen into a disaster area trying to fix them himself or he'd slip outside to play in the snow until Pete finally ventured into the kitchen to make them for him. The kid was good and usually listened to a direct order, unless it happened to bump up against his own exuberance.

Sure enough, when Pete got to the kitchen, Davey was on a chair, the box of mix upside down over a bowl. He'd poured in enough to feed an army battalion.

"Whoa, kid! Let's not get carried away," Pete said, extracting the box from his hands and putting it back in the cabinet. "How about setting the table? You remember how to do it?"

"Yeah, but how come it has to be all fancy when it's just us?"

"It's not fancy to put silverware and a napkin where they belong. Knowing where things like that go will impress a girl someday."

Davey stared at him blankly. "How come?"

"It's just one of those rules of life, pal. Girls like things done a certain way. When guys understand that, life goes a whole lot more smoothly."

Davey shook his head, his expression still perplexed. "Dad, you're weird."

"Maybe, but you love me, right?" Pete asked, scooping him up and holding him upside down till he squealed.

"I love you. I love you," Davey said, squirming till Pete set him back on his feet.

"Then set the table."

Davey did as he was told, but even after Pete put the first batch of pancakes in front of him, he was bouncing in his chair, clearly eager to be finished and outside.

"How deep do you think it is?" he asked Pete.

"Maybe if it were light enough to see outside, I could tell you."

"It's almost light," Davey argued.

"How can you tell?"

"Way over there, where you told me to look, you can see a tiny little bit of light right at the bottom. And pretty soon, it will turn all red and streaky and stuff and then, bam, the sun will come up."

Pete grinned at him. "I guess you've got this sunrise stuff nailed, after all."

"That's 'cause you taught me." Davey's expression suddenly turned solemn. "You always teach me really cool stuff. Mom teaches me spelling and words and things, but the things you tell me about are way better."

Pete knew it was Davey's way of broaching a subject that had come up in the past. He wanted to spend more time with Pete and didn't get why he couldn't. Pete refused to get drawn into a debate of the merits of Kelsey's lessons versus his own. Nor did he want to explain yet again that their time together had been spelled out by the court.

Instead, he met his son's gaze. "Spelling and words are important, pal. Don't ever forget that."

"So is how to hammer a nail and where the sun comes up," Davey retorted.

"And how to set a table," Pete added. "Let's not forget that."

Davey rolled his eyes and climbed out of his chair. "Can we go outside yet?"

"I've barely taken the first bite of my pancakes, much less had my first cup of coffee," Pete protested, then relented. "Bundle up and go on out, but stay right by the house. I'll be out in a little while and we can go build that fort."

"How come we can't build it here?"

"Because I know a better place."

"But we don't have to wait long to go there, right?"

"No," Pete assured him. "We don't have to wait long."

Just until he got sufficient caffeine in his system to guarantee he could keep up with his son.

Chapter Twelve

Not that she was eager or anything, but Jo was over at Pete's house by the bay twenty minutes ahead of the agreed-upon time. As she sat in her car with the heater blasting, she studied the snow-covered landscape and knew, once again, that she simply had to live here. It was like a fairyland now that the sun had come up and the ground and trees were sparkling as if they'd been dusted with diamonds overnight.

Seeing it like this gave her some new ideas about what ought to be planted—holly trees with their dark green leaves and bright red berries certainly, and perhaps a grove of pine trees and blue spruce that would look like something on a Christmas card on mornings like this. Most properties around here couldn't afford the space for an entire grove of trees, but Pete had bought up at least two acres. He'd only cleared a small portion of that facing the water.

Jo was lost in a sketch of the proposed grove, when she was startled by a tap on the window of her car. She turned to find Pete grinning at her and beside him a pint-sized replica bundled into a bright red jacket with blue mittens on his hands and a knitted blue cap pulled low over his ears. He was frowning at her.

"You're trespassing," he announced when she rolled down her window. "This is my dad's house."

Pete started to say something, but Jo stopped him.

"You must be Davey," she said, fighting the sting of tears as she looked into that precious face with its startling blue eyes and freckled nose.

His frown only deepened. "How come you know that? I don't know you."

"Because your dad told me how handsome and smart his son was, so that has to be you." She slid out of the truck and held out her hand. "I'm Jo. I'm doing some work for your dad."

Davey stared at her hand, clearly torn between suspicion and every lesson he'd ever been taught about being polite to grown-ups. He finally gave her hand a reluctant shake, though the scowl still hadn't left his face.

"What kind of work?" he asked, his voice laced with skepticism. "Girls don't build things."

"Uh-oh," Pete muttered, clearly amused at the sexist controversy his son had just unwittingly opened up.

Jo grinned at Davey. Six definitely wasn't too early to start teaching a kid about equality. "Is that so? Who told you that? Not your father, I'll bet."

"Definitely not me," Pete acknowledged hurriedly.

"Your mom, then?" Jo asked Davey.

He suddenly looked a little less sure of himself. "Nah. She always says girls can do anything boys can do."

"She's absolutely right," Jo said, surprised to find herself siding with Kelsey Catlett about anything. "Then who gave you the ridiculous notion that girls can't build anything?"

The smart kid promptly turned the tables on her. "Have you ever built anything?"

"In a way."

"Like what?"

"I design gardens and then I put them together for people. That's why I'm here. I'm designing some things for this house. Want to see?"

Clearly intrigued, he nodded and inched closer when she pulled her pad out of the car. She flipped it open to the page she'd just completed. Davey's eyes widened.

"Wow!" he said. "It's like Christmas!"

Jo beamed at him. "That was exactly my idea."

"Where's it gonna go?"

"If your dad agrees, I thought right about there," she said gesturing toward an open spot on this side of the house that wouldn't block any of the water views. Instead, it would offer a completely contrasting view to anyone sitting in the dining room having breakfast on a morning like this one. Turning one way, they'd see the bay. Facing the other, they'd look into a small forest of evergreens. Either view would provide a tranquil backdrop for their morning coffee.

"Are you gonna do it, Dad?" Davey asked excitedly. "It would be so cool to have Christmas trees growing right outside. We could even put lights on 'em at Christmas. We'd look outside and it would be like a fairyland."

Pete grinned at him indulgently, then faced Jo. "I guess that's a yes on the trees. Anything else in that notebook of yours?"

She handed it to him. "It's more like notes right now. I drove around yesterday to get some ideas. I haven't worked them into any sort of plan yet."

With Davey tugging on his arm begging to see, Pete knelt down so his son could look over his shoulder at the drawings. They lingered intently over each one. Jo watched Davey almost as intently as she did Pete and was pleased by the reactions she detected on their faces.

"Cool," Davey pronounced when they'd looked at every page. "Can you teach me to draw like that?"

"I'd love to," Jo said, thrilled by his eagerness and his apparent acceptance. She knew it could have been a whole lot harder to win him over. And maybe this was just détente.

"Now?" he asked.

"Hey, buddy, I thought you wanted to build a snow fort?"

"Oh, yeah," Davey said, readily distracted. He grinned up at Jo. "You want to help? Dad and me can show you how."

"I would love to help," she said. "Where are you going to build it?"

"By the water," Davey said at once. "That way when the bad guys come up by boat, we can nail 'em."

Jo laughed. "Good plan."

"The kid is definitely full of ideas," Pete said, tagging along behind them as Davey led the way to his chosen location.

Jo turned and met his gaze, hoping he could see the gratitude in her eyes for this chance. "Thank you," she mouthed silently.

When they finally reached the site for the fort, she turned to Davey. "Okay, Captain Catlett, what do we do first?"

Davey giggled. "First we make really big snowballs, right, Dad? Big as me."

Jo nodded thoughtfully. "Then who gets to lift them? Your dad?"

"He's really, really strong," Davey said with evident pride. "He could probably even lift you."

Jo chuckled. "I am definitely bigger than a giant snowball," she agreed, loving the way the boy's mind worked, to say nothing of his enthusiasm for whatever he set out to do. What an absolute joy he must be!

Oddly, she was feeling none of the anguish she'd expected to hit her when she first set eyes on him. She was simply gathering up every precious moment and storing it away to think about when he wasn't around. She wondered if that's how Pete survived the separations, by making so many memories that his son was never far from mind.

It took them two hours to build the fort to Davey's very precise specifications. Once it was done, Jo was the first to get behind the wall and lob a snowball straight at Pete. It hit him squarely in the chest, catching him completely by surprise. Jo ducked down behind the wall when he started to reach for his own fistful of snow.

While he was distracted, Davey hurled another one that he barely managed to duck.

"Okay, you two, this is war," Pete declared, pelting them with snowballs of his own, then chasing down Davey and rubbing snow on his neck.

Next he came after Jo, a diabolical expression in his eyes, but she was quick. She whirled away and ran, laughing as she danced out of his path.

The laughter died, when he snagged her ankle, somehow managing to land beneath her, so that he took the brunt of the fall. She grinned down at him. "You are such dead meat," she said, picking up a handful of snow to rub in his face.

But before she could do that, a fistful of snow was shoved down the back of her jacket by his sneaky little boy, whom she'd mistakenly assumed to be on her side. She should have known better.

"Way to go, Davey!" Pete enthused, giving his son a high five. "We guys have to stick together."

Laughing, Jo got up to shake the snow out of her jacket. "I'll remember this," she warned Pete. "Just wait."

His gaze locked on hers. "You gonna get even, tough girl?"

"You bet," she said at once. "And you won't even see it coming."

"Uh-oh," Davey said, grinning at his dad. "You're in big trouble, huh?"

Pete winked at him. "Nothing I can't handle."

Jo laughed at the pair of them. "Okay, macho guys, let's go have lunch before we all catch pneumonia. Soup and burgers? How about it?"

"With fries?" Davey asked at once.

"If your dad agrees," she told him.

"He will," Davey said triumphantly. "Dad loves fries better than anything."

He always had, Jo thought, and barely managed to keep herself from saying it aloud.

"Not better than anything," Pete replied quietly, his intense gaze fastened on Jo. "Some things are even more incredible."

Jo lost herself in the heat in his eyes for a moment, but then the moment was lost when Davey demanded to know what could possibly be any better than French fries.

Pete tugged his blue cap a little lower to cover his eyes. "Kissing girls," he said at once, then stole one from Jo before Davey could rip away the impromptu blindfold.

His son regarded him with blatant skepticism. "Gross," he declared.

"Tell me that when you're sixteen," Pete said. "Hop into the truck, buddy. I'll be there in a minute as soon as I open the car door for Jo."

"Can't she open it herself?" Even as the words left his mouth, Davey's expression brightened with sudden understanding. "It's another one of those things to keep girls happy, huh?"

Pete winked at him. "Exactly."

Davey ran on to the truck, while Pete went with Jo and opened the door.

"See you in ten minutes in town," he said.

"Do you think it's going okay?" she asked worriedly.

"Are you kidding? The kid's fallen in love with you," he said. "Same as me."

He winked and left, leaving her with her heart thundering in her chest and a million and one dreams coming alive again.

Lunch was an unqualified success. Pete watched his son with the woman who should have been the mother of Pete's children and knew that they could become the perfect family. Jo was a natural with the boy and Davey was responding to her effortless teasing with increasing affection. He told himself he wasn't leaving Kelsey out of the equation, just adding Jo into it, but it was hard to imagine Kelsey fitting in to the idyllic image in his head.

"Hey, Dad, I have an idea," Davey said, when they were all stuffed with hamburgers, fries and slices of pie. "You said we could rent a movie tonight. Maybe Jo could come, too. It would be like a party. You could make popcorn and hot chocolate and stuff."

Pete grinned at him. "Maybe Jo doesn't like popcorn and hot chocolate and silly kid movies."

"Bet she does," Davey said confidently. "Right, Jo? You think all that stuff is cool, don't you?"

"Nothing better," she agreed at once. "*Finding Nemo* was one of my all-time favorite movies."

"See," Davey said. "So, can we ask her?"

Pete laughed. "I think you just did."

Davey gave him a baffled look, then grinned. "Oh, yeah. So, will you come, Jo?"

She cast a look at Pete, clearly seeking his permission. "What do you say, Dad?"

"Fine with me," he said at once. He glanced at his

son. "Maybe we should let her pick the movie. What do you think?"

Davey looked doubtful. "You aren't gonna pick some mushy thing, are you?"

"Nah," she said at once. "How about I show you my choices and you can help me decide?"

Davey nodded eagerly, then glanced worriedly at Pete. "That sounds fair, right, Dad?"

"More than fair," he said with amusement.

He wasn't sure who was manipulating whom anymore. It was just plain as day that these two knew how to work each other. It couldn't have made him happier, but it was worrisome, too. The instantaneous bonding was going to cause problems down the road. Kelsey would hear all about this, and there would be hell to pay. But Pete had accepted that going in. Sooner or later, his ex-wife would have to come to terms with the fact that he really had moved on. He knew it would dash the hopes he suspected she had that one day he would come to his senses and chase after her.

"Okay, let's head for the video store and pick out a couple of movies, one for tonight and one for tomorrow. Then Davey and I can run by the store for supplies."

"Sounds good," Jo said.

"You want to come by around six-thirty and have dinner with us? We're going with the canned spaghetti thing," he told her with a grin.

"I think I'll pass, unless you can be persuaded to sacrifice the canned stuff in favor of homemade. I still have sauce in the freezer."

"Awesome," Davey said at once.

Jo slapped his hand in a high five. "There's the man," she said approvingly.

"Okay, then, I guess dinner's under control," Pete said.

"I'd better come at six, though, to boil the pasta and heat up the sauce."

Pete nodded. "We have a plan, then."

It was the kind of plan he'd always imagined making on a snowy Saturday with his family, but Kelsey had always insisted that Saturday was a date night, not a family night. She didn't care where they went, as long as it was out and they were alone. He looked into Jo's shining eyes and saw no hint of hesitation or dismay. If anything, she looked as eager as his son.

How had he ever for a single second forgotten that she was the perfect match for him? Okay, if he was being totally honest, he hadn't forgotten. He'd just buried the knowledge in order to live the life he'd been forced to choose.

And now, at long last, he had a second chance. He vowed here and now that he wouldn't waste it.

It was nearly midnight when Jo finally got home from their outing. She was on such an emotional high, she didn't think it was possible that she'd ever come back to earth. The spaghetti had been a big success with Davey, as had her special hot chocolate with just a hint of peppermint in it. They'd eaten a huge bowl of buttered popcorn and watched both movies, though Davey had fallen asleep fifteen minutes into the second one. Pete had carried him to bed, then returned to snuggle with her in front of the TV.

Neither of them had paid much attention to the plot of the movie, which was probably just as well, since she assumed Pete was destined to see it again on Sunday night when Davey realized he'd slept through most of it.

Tonight had been bittersweet. It had given her a taste of all she'd lost…and maybe all she could have, if she was brave enough to take another chance on loving Pete.

Was she that brave? She was beginning to believe she was, but now and then a vague feeling of panic would roll over her. At its core was always the faceless woman who'd stolen Pete from her the first time. Kelsey still had a powerful claim on him. Something told Jo that she wouldn't give it up lightly. Worse, Davey was bound to be caught in the middle. Pete didn't seem to be half as worried about that as she was, but she knew she could never do anything that might turn that wonderful child into some sort of pawn between his parents.

Too wound up to sleep, she made herself a cup of chamomile tea, then sat at the kitchen table, wishing for once that her sisters were here to listen to her jumbled thoughts and help her make sense of them. Unfortunately, if she told them everything now, she had a feeling not one of them would see Pete for the incredible man he was. They would focus exclusively on the fact that he'd broken her tender young heart.

When the phone rang, she almost laughed. It was bound to be Ashley, checking up on her, putting her mind at rest that Jo had survived her day with Pete and his son without any emotional scars.

"Hello, worrywart," she said, when she picked up.

"How'd you know it would be me?" Pete asked.

"Actually I was sure it was going to be Ashley. I thought you'd be sound asleep by now."

"I couldn't sleep till I knew you were home safe and in bed. Are you in bed?" he asked hopefully.

"Nope, fully dressed and in the kitchen. Sorry to spoil your fantasy."

"Ah, well, I have a pretty vivid imagination anyway. I'll make do."

"Today was fun," she told him quietly. "Thank you."

"It was fun for me, too, and Davey was over the moon. Of course, he'll never be satisfied to eat spaghetti from a can again."

"An educated palate is never a bad thing," she told him.

"I'll add that to the list of lessons I can take credit for," he said lightly. "'Night, darlin'."

"Good night, Pete."

It was fully a minute before Jo finally hung up the phone and cut the connection. She sighed when it rang again.

Smiling, she picked it up. "I thought we'd said good night, Pete."

"So that's who you were on the phone with," Ashley said. "Didn't you just leave him?"

"You're up late," Jo commented, ignoring her sister's testy tone.

"I wasn't waiting up for you to get home, if that's what you're thinking. Josh and I had to go to some big dinner-dance thing with his old law partners in Richmond tonight. We just got back. Thought I'd check on you before going to bed, but your line was busy."

"How was the event you went to?"

"Boring," Ashley said. "I'd almost forgotten how dull a roomful of lawyers can be."

"Oh, my God," Jo said with exaggerated alarm. "Let me check outside to see if the sky is falling."

"Very funny. How was your date with Pete and his son?"

"Amazing," Jo admitted. "And scary."

"Scary? Why?"

"I love that kid," she admitted. "Now the stakes have really gotten high, Ashley. I want them both in my life. I'm not sure if I'll be able to handle it if I lose them."

"Why would you lose them?"

"It could happen," Jo insisted. It was something she knew only too well.

"Do you want me to have the guys take Pete out and have the honorable intentions talk?"

The very idea filled Jo with horror. "Absolutely not."

"It's one way to get answers," Ashley reminded her.

"I think I'll use my own technique, thank you very much."

"You have a technique?"

"Well, no," she admitted. "Unless you count leaving it up to fate."

"Normally I'd be the first to tell you to forget that and take charge of your own future," Ashley said.

"But?"

"I'd have to say destiny's done all right by the rest of us, wouldn't you?"

Jo chuckled. "You have a point. Maybe I will just trust in fate."

"You might want to toss in some mind-boggling sex to seal the deal," Ashley suggested tartly. "Worked for me."

"I'm sure Pete would appreciate that technique," Jo agreed. "I'll give it some thought."

"Just be happy," Ashley said. "If you think that man can make you happy, then fight like heck to keep him."

Ashley's words continued to ring in Jo's head long after she'd hung up. That was the big difference between seven years ago and now. Back then, she hadn't known how to fight for her man, hadn't even known until too late that she needed to. Now, though, she was all grown up and stronger than she'd realized. This time she would fight with everything in her to hold on to the happiness she'd found once again with Pete.

And heaven help anyone who got in her way.

Chapter Thirteen

It was barely seven in the morning when Jo's phone rang. Sure that it would be Pete, she already had a smile on her face as she answered. When she heard Davey's voice, her smile spread even wider.

"Well, good morning," she said, instantly cheerful despite the early hour. "How are you?"

"I'm great," he said, his voice brimming with exuberance. "I wanted to call you before, but Dad said it was too early and that we had to wait till at least seven, so we wouldn't wake you. I know it's not quite seven, but I couldn't wait anymore. So, did we? Wake you up, I mean?"

Jo laughed. "No. I was awake."

"See, Dad? I told you it wouldn't be too early," Davey called out triumphantly to his father.

Jo couldn't hear Pete's mumbled response, but grinned as she imagined his side of the exchange. She could practically see the tolerant amusement on his face.

"Dad says to ask you if you want to go have waffles with us," Davey said. "He can't make waffles, 'cause you need some kind of iron thing, which is dumb, if you ask me, 'cause waffles aren't smooth."

Jo laughed. "It is dumb, now that you mention it. Are waffles a favorite of yours?"

"They're the best," Davey confirmed. "Even better than pancakes, 'cause there are all those little places for the syrup to go. So, will you come? Dad says we can come get you."

"How soon?"

He relayed her question at his father, then said, "He says twenty minutes. Can you be ready then?"

"I'll be ready," Jo promised.

"With your coat on and everything?" Davey asked worriedly. "I'm starving."

"I'll even be waiting outside," she assured him. "We definitely can't have you starving."

"Okay. Bye," he said, then put the phone down with a clatter.

Jo stared at the receiver, a smile on her lips, then finally hung up and raced to put on a little makeup and do something with her hair before her allotted time was up.

She was outside in the driveway when Pete turned in. He frowned at her as she got into the truck.

"Why are you standing outside?" he scolded. "It's freezing. You should have waited till we pulled in before coming out."

She winked at Davey. "I promised not to hold things up."

Pete turned to the backseat and frowned at his son. "You don't make girls stand around in the cold for your convenience," he chided.

"Are we gonna waste time while you tell me another one of those things about keeping girls happy?" Davey asked plaintively. "It's going to be years and years before I need to know that stuff."

Pete regarded him with resignation. "Have you gotten the message?"

"Yes," Davey said at once. "Can we please go now?"

"Yes, please," Jo added. "I'm starving, too."

Pete laughed. "Something tells me this breakfast is going to cost me a fortune. Hope I have enough cash."

"I have my allowance," Davey said. "I can pay for my own."

"How about mine?" Pete retorted. "Can you pay for mine, too?"

Davey immediately reached in his pocket and brought out a fistful of dollars and some change. He shoved it in Jo's direction. "Is this enough?"

She solemnly counted out his four dollars and sixty-seven cents, then shook her head. "Not quite," she told him. "But don't worry. I've got it covered."

"Girls don't pay," he responded at once. "Right, Dad?"

"That's right," Pete confirmed.

"It's okay for girls to pay for things some of the time," Jo corrected. "But it's always nice when the guys offer."

Davey regarded her with confusion. "How am I supposed to know when it's okay?"

Jo laughed at his perplexed expression. "Sweetie, it is not something you need to worry about for at least ten years or so."

"I don't think I'm ever gonna need it," Davey said. "It's probably easier just to stay away from girls."

"Easier, maybe," his dad said, clearly amused. "But not nearly as much fun. You'll see."

"I doubt it," Davey said with blatant skepticism as Pete pulled into a parking spot in front of the café in town.

When the three of them walked through the door, a half-dozen curious glances were directed their way. People spoke to Pete and grinned at Davey, but faltered a bit when they came to Jo. She was relieved when they were finally seated in a booth toward the back. She hadn't stopped to think about how awkward this might turn out to be. Naturally, most people here had known Kelsey. Many of them might have a vague recollection of Jo, but after seven years they obviously didn't recognize her as the young girl who'd spent an entire summer coming in here with Pete.

At least none picked up on the connection until the waitress came to take their order. She'd worked here for years and took one look at Jo and beamed. "Jo D'Angelo, if you aren't a sight for sore eyes. It's been a long time, girl. I see your sisters in here all the time these days, but you've been keeping yourself scarce. Heard you were with them once, but I missed you. Glad you're finally back, though I can't see that your taste in men has improved much over the years." She grinned at Pete when she said it.

Jo laughed. "Hello, Gloria. I just came down recently to stay at Rose Cottage for a bit."

The waitress immediately looked disappointed. "You're not moving here?"

"I haven't decided yet," Jo said, ignoring Pete's stunned expression.

After the woman had gone to place their order, Pete looked at Jo. "What did that mean? I thought you'd pretty much decided to stick around."

She used his obvious dismay to sneak in another play for his house. "Maybe if I had the perfect house…" she said and let her voice trail off.

He shook his head. "Don't you pull that on me," he scolded. "Don't make me responsible for your going or staying."

Jo simply stared at him, letting the words sink in. Even though they'd been spoken lightly, she doubted he realized how telling they were. It was a warning, in fact, one she would do well not to ignore. If she stayed here, it had to be all about her and what she wanted, not about what might or might not happen with Pete. She'd very nearly forgotten that in the warm glow of being with him—and with Davey—these past couple of days. Her spirits, so high when she'd left Rose Cottage, took a nosedive.

When the waffles came, they might just as well have been sawdust. Even though Pete was watching her with a worried look, she barely managed to choke down more than a few bites. Even Davey seemed to notice that something was wrong. He fell silent and concentrated on his breakfast, finishing his own waffle in record time.

"Can I go outside?" he begged his father.

Before Pete could reply, Jo said, "If your dad's not finished, I'll come with you."

"He can go by himself," Pete countered. "I think we should talk."

"Not here and not now," she said just as firmly, already scooting out of the booth and pulling on her jacket.

"But you didn't eat. You said you love waffles and that you were as hungry as me," Davey said. "Did you get sick?"

"No," she assured him. At least not the way he meant. She held out her hand. "Maybe we can walk to the park and build a snowman. What do you say, Davey?"

His concern for her mood vanished at once. "Cool. Is it okay, Dad?"

Pete looked as if he wanted to argue, but he finally relented. "I'll meet you there in a few minutes," he said, his voice tight.

On the way to the park, Jo was grateful for Davey's nonstop chatter. And once they were there, she forced herself to concentrate on helping him build a snowman. Since the temperature had risen slightly once the sun came out, the snow was melting fast now. The poor snowman wasn't nearly as plump as he should have been. He looked about as defeated and sad as she felt. Not even the curved stick Davey found to use as a mouth could perk him up. The makeshift smile looked forced.

How had things turned upside down in less than twenty-four hours? Jo wondered. This time yesterday, she'd been filled with joy and hope. Now it was as if she'd run headlong into reality, all because of a few careless words that Pete had spoken, probably half in jest.

While Davey scrambled through the park looking for more sticks to create arms and something to use for eyes and a nose, Jo sat on a nearby bench and watched. She released a sigh when Pete sat down next to her, his expression troubled.

"Mind telling me what happened back there?" he asked quietly. "One minute everything was fine and you had a smile on your face, the next you looked as if you'd caught me kicking your dog."

She could have lied and pretended that nothing had happened, but he would never buy it, not after she'd all but walked out on him. She might as well admit to the truth.

"You said something that reminded me that all this is just temporary."

He stared at her blankly. "You were the one who said you were only here for a while, not me. What did I say?"

"That you couldn't be responsible for my decision to stay or go." She met his shocked gaze. "And you were right. It has to be about me. All of this…" She waved a hand to encompass him and Davey. "It's not mine."

"I was just teasing you about the house," Pete said, clearly contrite. "I thought you knew that."

"I know that's what you intended," she agreed. "But there was an underlying truth that I can't ignore."

"Underlying truth," he repeated as if it were a foreign concept. "I only say what I mean, Jo. There was no underlying truth or undercurrent or hidden meaning. That's a female thing."

She shot a sharp look at him. "You really don't want to go there."

"I just meant that you can count on whatever I say. I don't have hidden agendas."

She gave him a sad look. "I used to believe that. Now

I know that I have to listen to what you don't say as much as what you do."

"And you got all this from some stupid comment I made as a joke?" he asked, clearly exasperated.

"Yes."

"Well, listen to this, then," he said heatedly, grasping her shoulders and pulling her close, then claiming her mouth with a ferocity that sucked the breath right out of her lungs.

Only after what seemed like an eternity did the kiss gentle before ending on a sigh. His. Maybe hers.

He gazed deep into her eyes. "Did you hear what I was saying then?"

Shaken, she nodded. She hadn't needed words to get that particular message.

"What? Say it, so I can be sure we're on the same page about that much at least."

"That you want me."

He shoved a hand through his hair. "And that's all?" he asked with evident frustration. "You just felt the wanting?"

She nodded.

"Not the love?"

Oh, how she wanted to believe in the love, but she couldn't let herself. "No," she said softly. "Not the love."

Pete regarded her wearily. "Then, darlin', I think you might want to consider the possibility that you're tone-deaf, if all you can hear is what might tear us apart, instead of the one thing that will keep us together."

He stood up, called to Davey, then gave her another of those weary looks. "I'll take you home now. Give you some time to think."

Jo nodded. "That's probably best," she said, though being home alone with her thoughts was the last thing she really wanted.

When Davey came up, he studied them both worriedly. "Are you guys fighting?"

Jo forced a smile. "No."

"Yes," Pete said, then ruffled his son's hair. "But we'll settle it. That's a promise."

"I hope so," Davey said, his gaze on Jo. "'Cause I want you to spend time with me and Dad next time I come."

"If I'm here, it's a date," Jo promised.

But if she had even half a grain of sense left in her head, she'd make sure to be long gone.

For the first time in the two years that he and his son had been separated, Pete regretted the boy's presence. He wanted to settle this thing with Jo before it got all blown out of proportion and she did something they'd both regret. But he knew he simply had to backburner that conversation until he got back from Richmond on Monday. It made the rest of Sunday and the trip down to Kelsey's drag out like water torture.

They were halfway down there when Davey announced, "Dad, I've been thinking."

"About?"

"Jo."

He glanced over at his son. "Oh?"

"I think she's mad at us."

"Not us, kiddo. Me."

"How come?"

"I'm not entirely sure, but I'll straighten it out."

"And she'll be there when I come back?"

"Yes," Pete said. She would be there, no matter what he had to do to guarantee it. "You really liked her, didn't you?"

"Uh-huh."

"What did you like about her?" he asked curiously. Pete knew what *he* loved—her strength, her humor, her gentleness—but those weren't the things that would appeal to a six-year-old.

Davey's expression turned thoughtful. "Well, she's pretty and all that, but I liked it best that she didn't care about getting all messed up. She played with me and just had fun. Mom's always worried about her hair and stuff."

Pete sighed. He didn't want Davey to start making this kind of comparison. "There's nothing wrong with your mom wanting to look nice."

"I know," Davey replied. "But there's nothing wrong with having fun, either."

"No," Pete agreed. "No, there's not."

He was still thinking about that when he got back home that night. Jo had brought fun back into both their lives. He wasn't going to let that go without a fight, especially not over some silly argument he didn't entirely understand. Underlying truths be damned, he thought viciously. He intended to talk to her in plain English until she got how much he loved her.

But before he could call her, he noticed that the answering machine light was blinking like crazy. He pressed the button for messages as he took off his jacket.

"We need to talk," Kelsey announced, her tone petulant. "Who is this woman that Davey was going on and on about? Call me the minute you get in."

Pete sighed. He'd anticipated this. Kelsey hated him interfering in her social life, but she had no such qualms about involving herself in his. And it went without saying that Davey would inadvertently get her all riled up with his glowing remarks about the new woman in Pete's life.

Up till now, there hadn't been many opportunities for her to ask questions. The few women he'd dated since the divorce had merely been passing through. Because of that, he'd kept them away from his son. He hadn't wanted Davey to go through some perpetual cycle of attachment and loss the way he had as a boy.

He'd broken that rule with Jo. Though she was still cautious with him—more than cautious, if yesterday was anything to go by—*he* knew she was in his life to stay. He wanted her and his son to get to know each other and to get along.

Until this moment, listening to his ex-wife's tone, he'd been ecstatic at how well the weekend had gone. Jo and Davey had taken to each other at once. It had never occurred to Pete to tell Davey not to mention Jo to his mother. Even if it had, he wouldn't have done it. Teaching a kid to keep secrets from one parent or another just to keep the peace was flat-out wrong.

Based on the six messages that were more of the same and because he knew his ex-wife would only keep calling until she got the answers she wanted, he grabbed a bottle of beer from the fridge and called her back.

"What's up?" he asked, as if she hadn't already made that plain in her message.

"Who's Jo?"

"A friend."

"I thought you said you weren't going to parade your women in front of Davey."

He bit back a sharp retort about her parade of men through their son's life. "For starters, I don't have a lot of women in my life, so there's never going to be a parade."

She hesitated, then asked, "What's different about this one?"

Before he could answer, she gasped. "Oh my God, Jo—she's the one, isn't she? Jo's the reason our marriage fell apart. Jo, what was her name? Something Italian. D'Angelo? That's it. Is that who you were with this weekend? The woman who broke up our marriage?"

Pete was stunned by the totally unfounded accusation. "What the hell are you talking about, Kelsey? Our marriage fell apart because you were unhappy. You didn't want to stay here, and I wouldn't move."

"I didn't want to stay there because I knew you were still in love with someone else and that everything in that stupid place was a reminder of her. The whole town knew I was your second choice."

Pete clamped a tight lid on his temper. "You're revising history, Kelsey. I did everything I could think of to make our marriage work. I never once threw some other woman in your face."

"But she was there just the same," she insisted stubbornly. "Don't you think I knew all about your sweet little summer romance with that girl from Boston? The whole county knew about it. Even when we made love, I knew she was in your head. You couldn't stop talking about her. The two of you were sickening."

"And yet you couldn't wait to sleep with me," he reminded her.

"I wasn't in that bed alone, hot stuff," she reminded him. "You didn't put up much of a fight."

Pete sighed. He hated it, but there was no denying what she said. Rehashing it again wasn't going to get them anywhere. "Kelsey, all of that happened a long time ago. It doesn't matter now."

"It does if she's the woman you introduced to our son. I won't have it, Pete," she said heatedly. "I won't allow you to humiliate me like that. It was bad enough that everyone in town knew about her, that they knew you'd only married me because of the baby."

"How am I humiliating you?" he asked, genuinely baffled by her spin on his relationship with Jo. "We've been divorced for a couple of years now. How many men have you introduced into Davey's life? Have I ever suggested that you're doing it to humiliate me? My only complaint is when you neglect him while you're courting your latest conquest."

"This is different," she insisted. "This Jo is the woman who came between us."

"I think you have that backward," he said. "The truth is that you're the woman who came between me and Jo. That was my fault, and I took responsibility for it. When you got pregnant, I married you."

"Only out of obligation," she repeated.

"Yes," he said, seeing little point in sugarcoating the truth when they both knew it. "But I wanted it to work, Kelsey. I gave it my all. You can't possibly deny that."

"Really? How many times were you thinking of her when we made love? Don't you think I knew that? You'd get this faraway, sad look in your eyes, and I always knew you wished I was her."

The conversation was spinning wildly out of control, and Pete was tired of it. She wouldn't believe anything he said anyway, not when she was in this bitter, accusatory mood.

"I've got to go," he said. "We'll discuss this some other time."

"I won't let you see Davey if you insist on having her around," she threatened.

It was the last straw. His temper snapped. "Don't you dare try to use that boy as a weapon," Pete retorted furiously. "Two can play at that game, Kelsey, and trust me, if I play, I'll play to win."

He hung up before she could reply to that, then threw the half-empty beer bottle across the room. It shattered against the wall, sending glass and golden liquid raining down.

"Pete?"

He turned to find Jo staring at him, her eyes wide with shock.

"I'm sorry," he said tightly. "I didn't know you were there."

"I just got here. I knocked, but when you didn't answer, I came on in. I hope that's okay."

"Yeah, sure," he said, raking a hand through his hair. "Why are you here?"

She regarded him hesitantly. "I came over because I thought we ought to talk, but if this is a bad time, that can wait. What on earth happened just now? Who were you yelling at?"

"Just a little chat with my ex-wife," he said, forcing a light note into his voice. "She knows how to push my buttons."

"Want to talk about it?"

"Absolutely not," he said flatly. "Now come here and kiss me."

She gave him a skeptical look. "Don't you think we should clean up the mess first?" She gestured toward the puddle of beer and broken glass. "That one, and the mess I made of things yesterday morning?"

He glanced at the glass and liquid on the floor. It could wait. So could the conversation, if her being here meant she was reconsidering that stupid underlying truth garbage. There was one way to find out.

"We could mop up the mess," he agreed. "Or we could go upstairs and make love. You tell me which sounds like more fun."

"Going upstairs, definitely," she said, but she still didn't move. Nor did she accept his outstretched hand. "But I think we should talk first. About what happened yesterday morning and about what happened just now. Something tells me the latter is even more important."

"Why?"

"Because it's real life, Pete. You can't protect me from the bad stuff. And I know you're still angry about what happened yesterday. Let's get it all out in the open. We can't heal things and move on if we don't face them."

"I'm not trying to protect you from anything," he said defensively.

She gave him a disbelieving look. "Do you honestly think I don't see that you're determined not to ever let anything hurt me again? You're trying to make up for what happened seven years ago. You want to push all of that into some hole and bury it, pretend it never happened."

"So what if I am? What's wrong with wanting you to be happy?"

"Nothing. I love you for trying, but unfortunately life simply can't be all smooth sailing. We have to be able to weather all of it."

"We're not making love, are we?" he asked, resigned.

She grinned at him. "Not just yet. You pick up the glass, and I'll get some soapy water to clean up the mess."

"You know that's the symptom, not the issue, don't you?"

"Of course, but you can tell me all about it while we work."

He laughed at the idea that he could explain it all so easily. "It's not that big a mess. It won't take that long to clean it up."

She studied him quizzically. "Is it such a big issue, then?"

He snagged her hand and pulled her into his arms, then rested his chin on her head. "It could be, if we let it turn into one."

"Then we won't let it," she said simply.

He gazed into her eyes, surprised. Her doubts of the day before seemed to have vanished. "Easy as that?"

"If we face it together," she said at once. "That's what I was going to tell you. That's the conclusion I reached."

And seeing the confidence and love shining in her eyes, Pete was almost able to convince himself that she was right. And so he sat down, pulled her onto his lap and told her about his fight with Kelsey.

Jo had never let herself think that much about Pete's ex-wife. She hadn't wanted to think about the woman who'd stolen him away from her. Not that Pete was blameless. They'd acknowledged that and moved on.

But Kelsey Prescott Catlett was some faceless woman who was no longer a part of his life, beyond her role as the mother of his child. That's the way Jo wanted to keep it. She could see, after listening to Pete, that it wasn't going to be that easy.

"She sounds jealous," she said when he was through.

"Don't be ridiculous."

"What do you think is behind her reaction?" she asked.

He considered the question, his expression thoughtful, then shrugged. "Okay, she's jealous, but that's absurd. She wanted the divorce. She's been dating ever since she got to Richmond. Why, all of a sudden, is she all bent out of shape about me having someone in my life."

"Because it's me," she said simply. "I suppose I can't really blame her. It's another one of those reality checks like the one that got to me on Sunday. We have to deal with them, Pete. They're not going to go away."

He gave her a questioning look. "But I thought you were."

"A momentary panic attack," she said.

"How'd you get over it?"

"I tried to imagine my life without you in it. I couldn't." Saying that made her vulnerable, which terrified her, but it was the truth. He needed to know it.

"Make me a promise, darlin'."

"Anything."

"If you ever feel one of these panic attacks coming on again, talk to me. Don't ever just turn tail and run."

Jo nodded. It was an easy promise to make, because she'd made it to herself only a few days ago. Somehow, on Sunday morning she'd lost track of that. It wouldn't happen again.

"Come here and kiss me," she said, fisting her hand in his shirt and dragging him toward her. "That'll help me remember the promise, if we seal it with a kiss."

He grinned. "Always happy to oblige, when it involves kissing you. Do you think you'll need reminding often?"

She chuckled at his hopeful expression. "Only about a hundred times a day."

He grinned. "It's going to be damn hard getting any work done at that rate, but I'll give it my best."

"You always do," Jo said right before his lips met hers and the world went spinning.

Chapter Fourteen

Jo couldn't seem to shake the image of walking into Pete's and hearing him on the phone in such a bitter argument with his ex-wife over her. She'd gone over there figuring she owed him a conversation about the whole incident on Sunday. She'd even had what she was going to say all planned out, but she hadn't expected to face a whole new quandary that seemed to turn her temporary moment of insanity into little more than a minor tempest.

She'd gotten scared, that was all. She'd let all her old fears and insecurities resurface in the blink of an eye, blown it all out of proportion and started an argument she hadn't known how to end. If she hadn't realized how stupid it was on her own, then walking in on Pete's argument with his ex-wife had shown her.

Those two had real issues, hurtful issues that could come between Jo and Pete, if they weren't very careful, if they weren't united. Ironically, having that common goal made their relationship stronger than ever. Jo doubted that Kelsey had considered that outcome before calling Pete to throw down the gauntlet.

Jo smiled as she thought of just how united she and Pete had been during the night. They'd definitely been in tune then. All their differences had been put behind them.

She'd awakened in his arms this morning, bounced out of his bed and gone happily off with a kiss to do more research for his landscaping projects. She wanted to finalize those plans with him soon, then talk to the local nursery owner about ordering the plants so they'd be in at the optimum time for planting in the spring.

Today it was even possible to believe that spring might be right around the corner. The sun had warmed things up to nearly sixty. The last of the snow had melted and she'd even spotted a couple of crocuses coming up in the garden at Rose Cottage. Daffodils were bound to be close behind. Perhaps that's why she was suddenly feeling so optimistic—maybe it was the natural exuberance of someone attuned to spring's symbolic evidence of rebirth and renewal. In her profession, the seasonal changes were something to be watched with appreciation and respect.

She came inside from her tour of Rose Cottage's garden feeling lighthearted. Maybe she'd even call Mike this afternoon and set up an appointment to talk about that partnership. It was time. She might as well admit that despite that little incident of self-doubt on Sunday, she wasn't going anywhere. Her future was here, hopefully with Pete, but if not, she knew she could be happy right here in Rose Cottage, which held so many joyous memories.

When the phone rang, Jo answered with a cheery greeting, only to have someone launch a venomous harangue that had her reaching for a chair to sit down. Her knees went weak and heat rose in her cheeks as she was called a litany of uncomplimentary names.

Kelsey, no doubt, she realized when her brain cells recovered from the initial shock of being verbally attacked and focused on the female voice, rather than the hateful words.

"I won't listen to this," she said quietly, interrupting the steady flow of venom. She hung up.

Naturally, the phone immediately rang again. She debated not answering, then decided to make at least one effort to turn it into a civilized, rational conversation. It was doubtful, but she couldn't ignore the opportunity to try to mend a few fences.

"Hello, Kelsey," she said, her voice as calm as she could make it when her nerves were a jittery mess. She was proud of the maturity and restraint she was capable of under these circumstances.

Apparently her recognition of the caller gave Kelsey pause. She was greeted with silence.

"If you want to talk about this calmly, that's one thing," Jo said, seizing the advantage she'd gained by catching the woman off guard. "But I won't listen to you spew all that garbage at me."

"You think you're so damn high and mighty, don't you?" Kelsey said heatedly. "You're nothing but a two-bit—"

Jo cut her off. "There you go again. I told you I wouldn't listen to that and I won't. Now, do we keep it civilized and try to work this out for your son's sake, or do I hang up again?"

"Don't you dare say a word about my son," Kelsey shouted. "You don't have the right. He's mine and I won't have you in his life, do you understand that?"

"I understand why you might prefer that, but you don't get your way on this one, Kelsey. If I'm with Pete, I will be spending time with Davey. He's a wonderful boy," she said, determined to take the high road until it fell off the edge of a probably inevitable cliff. "You've done an amazing job with him."

Kelsey was silent, probably grappling with how to react to hearing such a compliment from a woman she evidently despised. "I don't want you around my son," she said eventually.

"I can understand why you'd be concerned about that, but I promise you I won't do anything to interfere in your relationship. You're his mom, period."

"Aren't you hearing me? I said I don't want you anywhere near him. And stay away from Pete, too," Kelsey said. "You ruined our marriage, and I won't let you have him now."

"It's not up to you," Jo said patiently.

"Oh, really?" Kelsey replied with a bitter laugh. "Sweetheart, I'm holding all the cards. You had what? A couple of months with Pete when you were just a kid? I was with him for five years, as his *wife*."

"And yet you still don't know him," Jo retorted with quiet confidence.

"I know him well enough," Kelsey corrected. "I

know he will never do anything that might cost him his son."

"Of course not," Jo agreed.

"You could be the one who costs him Davey," Kelsey said coldly. "Which of you do you think he'll choose?"

Jo felt sick. How could this woman use her own child to threaten his father? But it was plain she wasn't above doing just that and turning all of the joy Jo and Pete had found into something ugly that could only tear them apart.

"I hope it won't come to that," Jo told her quietly. "I hope you care enough about your son that you'd never use him in that way. Davey loves both of you. Don't make *him* choose. It could backfire on you."

"Don't you dare suggest that you know more about my child than I do," Kelsey said furiously. "I hope you enjoyed that cozy little time you all spent together, because, trust me, it's going to have to last you forever."

This time, Kelsey was the one who hung up, leaving Jo shaking. Tears welled up in her eyes and streamed down her cheeks, because she knew that if push came to shove, she would walk away from Pete before she'd let that wonderful boy of his be hurt because of her.

And if that happened—*when* it happened, she thought fatalistically—it was going to break her heart.

Jo was still sitting at the kitchen table, her head aching from all the tears but her cheeks dry at last, when her sisters came through the door. Their timing couldn't have been any worse. One look at her and the fussing started.

"What did he do? What did that son of a bitch do to

you?" Ashley demanded, bringing her an unwanted glass of water, then pulling a chair right up beside her.

"It wasn't Pete," Jo told her emphatically. "At least not directly."

"I don't care if it was directly or indirectly, I won't let him get away with hurting you," Ashley declared. "I warned him. Heck, we all did."

Melanie placed a hand on Ashley's shoulder. "Maybe we should let Jo talk."

"Good idea," Maggie said, settling into a chair on Jo's other side.

"I don't know where to start," Jo told them. For them to understand, she needed to go all the way back to the beginning. She supposed it was way past time for her to do that.

"Take your time," Melanie said. "How about some soup first? Have you eaten?"

"I don't think so." She'd lost track of time, lost track of everything in the misery that had swamped her after Kelsey's threatening call. "But I'm not hungry."

"You need food." Melanie shot a warning look at Ashley. "Let's put the conversation on hold until you've eaten something."

Ashley frowned at her, but didn't argue, which Jo figured was testament to how awful she must look.

Everybody sat in silence and watched as she sipped the hot, homemade vegetable soup that Melanie had defrosted from one of the containers Maggie had left in the freezer.

"This is delicious," Jo said, wanting to end the awkward silence. "Will you teach me how to make it, Maggie?"

"Sure," Maggie said at once. "It's best if you use

fresh vegetables, but you can make it in no time if you use the packages of frozen vegetables."

"Are you finished yet?" Ashley demanded impatiently. "We're not here to swap recipes."

"Do you want some more?" Melanie inquired, giving Ashley another of those daunting looks that effectively silenced her, at least temporarily.

"No, I'm finished," Jo said with some regret. If she could have forced down another bite, she would have been able to postpone this conversation.

"Your color's better," Ashley noted.

"But there's still no sparkle in your eyes," Maggie commented. "What happened here today?"

"I got a call from Pete's ex-wife. Let's just say she's not happy with me and leave it at that."

"Where the hell does she get off calling you?" Ashley demanded. "If she has a problem, she needs to take it up with Pete."

"I couldn't agree more," Jo said. "And, believe me, she's made her unhappiness known to him, too."

"What did he have to say?"

"Last night, he told her to butt out. He doesn't know about what happened today. He doesn't know that she warned me she'll use Davey to come between us. She wants to force Pete to choose between his son and me."

To her relief, all three of her sisters looked totally scandalized by that.

"She doesn't stand a prayer in court," Ashley said. "If Pete needs help fighting her, tell him to come to me."

Jo regarded her with surprise. "You'd go to bat for him?"

"On something like that? Of course." She frowned. "Unless you don't want me to."

"No, of course not. I think it would be great. I just don't want it to come to that. It'll be better for everyone if they can work this out between the two of them without involving lawyers and a judge."

"Why is his ex-wife all of a sudden focusing on you?" Maggie asked.

"I guess Davey went home and told her about me and she went all weird and jealous." She debated not getting into the rest—into the past—but knew she'd feel better once the whole story was out there. "I almost think I understand some of what she's feeling."

Her sisters stared at her blankly. "You're sympathizing with her?"

"No," Jo said at once. "Not sympathizing, exactly." She sighed. "It's a long story."

"How long can it be?" Maggie asked. "You haven't known the man that long."

"Actually I have," Jo admitted. "I've known Pete for over seven years."

"Oh, my God," Melanie whispered softly, her eyes filled with sudden understanding. "He's the one."

"The one what?" Maggie asked.

"The one she was always hiding out from when she came down here while each of us was staying at Rose Cottage," Melanie said. She looked at Jo. "I'm right, aren't I? He's the person you were avoiding?"

Jo nodded. "I've been involved with Pete since I was eighteen years old," she finally admitted. "Or rather, I was involved with him that summer, and have been regretting it ever since because of how things turned out."

All three sisters stared at her as if she'd started babbling in some incomprehensible language.

"How?" Ashley asked.

"When?" Maggie chimed in.

Melanie frowned. "Wasn't he married?"

Jo scowled at her. "Of course he wasn't married when we met," she said. "But then he was, and that put an end to things."

By the time she'd explained it all, her sisters were staring at her with stunned expressions.

"And you never said a word," Ashley said. "I don't believe you could keep something this huge from us. Your first big romance and we never suspected a thing."

"You were all caught up in your own lives by then. And the whole pregnancy and marriage thing came up so soon after I got back to Boston that there was hardly any time to mention that I'd fallen in love before I would have had to say that he'd broken my heart."

"And then I had to go and hire him," Ashley said, her expression grim. "No wonder you were so furious with me."

"You didn't know," Jo said. "And it turns out that it was the best thing that could have happened. We've moved past all that, or past most of it, anyway."

"Then you've forgiven him? You trust him to do right by you now?" Maggie asked.

Jo nodded slowly. "Yes," she said quietly. "I think I do. But I can't be the kind of woman who gets between a man and his son, no matter how much I want a future with Pete. I could never have done it back then, even if he'd given me a choice, and I can't do it now."

Ashley gave her a look filled with resolve. "Then we

won't let it happen that way. Tell Pete about his ex-wife's call—and I mean every single vicious word of it—then tell him to come and see me if his wife doesn't start to see reason. I'm sure I can put a legal spin on things that will wake her up."

"Then you think there's still a chance for us to work this out?" Jo asked Ashley.

"Absolutely," her sisters said, obviously in total accord.

"If he's the one you want, then he's the one you should have," Melanie said. "And just to lock it in, I think I'll send Mike over here first thing in the morning to work out that business partnership."

"Maybe now's not the right time to do that," Jo protested. "Don't get me wrong. I want to do it and I want to stay here, but if things don't work out for me and Pete…"

"They will," Ashley assured her. "Have you ever known any of us not to get what we want when we fight for it together?"

A grin slowly spread across Jo's face. For the first time all afternoon, her heart felt lighter. "Now that you mention it, no."

"Then let's not even consider the possibility of ruining that track record," Ashley said, giving her an encouraging smile. "Deal?"

"Deal."

When Pete checked his messages at midafternoon, he had three from the D'Angelo sisters—one each from Ashley, Maggie and Melanie. But none from Jo. That alone told him that where he needed to be was Rose Cottage, and he didn't need any one of them telling him that. Something had happened, and the sisters were on the warpath. Even his answering service had gotten that much. Each message had been marked *URGENT.*

Pete called his secretary and had her reschedule the rest of his appointments and drove straight to Rose Cottage. When he knocked on the door, he wasn't sure what sort of response he expected, but it wasn't a woman who looked as if she'd spent most of the day crying and the rest trying to cover up the evidence.

"You're here," she said, looking surprised. "Who called you?"

"Ashley, Maggie and Melanie, in that order. They left messages. Since it had to be about you, I came here instead. What's going on?"

"I went a few rounds with Kelsey this morning," she said succinctly. "She called and shared her displeasure about our relationship."

Pete felt his blood begin to boil. "She did *what?*"

Jo summed up their conversation. "My sisters thought you ought to know what she's threatening. Ashley says she'll be happy to give you legal advice, if you want it. I'm still hoping it won't come to that." She lifted her gaze to meet his. "I'm so sorry. This is all my fault."

"How the hell is it your fault?" he asked heatedly. "This is Kelsey, start to finish. I'll handle her." He pressed a hard kiss to her lips. "You okay?"

She nodded, though he couldn't help thinking she still looked wounded. The only way to wipe that expression from her eyes, though, was to settle this with Kelsey once and for all. The urgency of that was the only thing that could have gotten him to leave Jo alone right now.

"Then I'm going to get this straightened out," he said with grim determination.

She regarded him with worry. "What are you going to do? You're not going down there and have some huge fight in front of your son, are you?"

Since that was precisely what Pete had intended, he faltered at the warning note in her voice. "No," he said retreating. "But I have to get through to her."

"Then make her come here. Tell her you need to talk and to get someone to look after Davey. Maybe he can stay with a friend tonight."

"I don't want her here," Pete countered. "I don't want her anywhere near you."

"She's not going to come near me, not when she has a chance to be with you. Come on, Pete. It's the only way."

"I suppose," he said skeptically. "Maybe we should have this meeting in your sister's office. That way Kelsey won't be able to misinterpret every word out of my mouth."

"Having a lawyer there, at least this first time, will only put her on the defensive. You have to try to work it out on your own."

Pete understood her logic, but the thought of actually inviting Kelsey to come here to talk made him nervous. He knew better than anyone just how easily she could misinterpret the overture.

But what could happen, really? It wasn't as if she could make something happen between them, not the way she'd managed to when he was twenty. He could control this meeting.

He tucked a finger under Jo's chin. "I'll call her," he said. "And I swear to you I will get this resolved tonight. Then you and I have a date, okay?"

"Let's not make any kind of plans just yet," she

pleaded. "Just keep all your focus on making this okay so you won't lose Davey."

"I'm not going to lose Davey," he said with finality.

Jo grinned at his conviction. "Then tomorrow morning we'll celebrate that," she promised.

"Eight o'clock? My place for pancakes?"

She slid into his embrace and held on tight. "My favorite way to start the day," she told him, her words muffled against his chest.

"Next to making love, mine, too," he said, smiling as he heard her chuckle.

"That goes without saying," she agreed, then lifted her gaze to his. "Make this work, Pete, please."

"I'll do my best, darlin'. That's a promise."

Even as he said it, though, he wondered if his promises meant a damn thing to her. He couldn't blame her if they didn't. So far, his track record wasn't exactly stellar.

Chapter Fifteen

Pete paced through the house he'd once shared with Kelsey, debating for the thousandth time if he'd made the right decision by asking her to come here. Too late now, though. She was on her way.

Instead of regretting the invitation, he needed to be planning what he was going to say to make her see reason. Unfortunately, he doubted there were sufficient words in the English language to make his ex-wife see past her own self-interest. He'd always known how self-absorbed she was, but her threats this morning only proved it.

It was nearly seven by the time he saw her headlights swing into the driveway, The knot in his gut twisted even tighter. He went and opened the door to avoid the awkward moment when she'd have to decide whether to ring the bell or walk right in. He was pretty sure he knew which she'd choose, if only to make a point that she still had a right to be here. Since she didn't make a habit of showing up, he'd never bothered to change the locks. Maybe he should do that just to make his own point.

"You made good time," he said when she got to the door.

"Rush hour traffic wasn't too bad, for a change."

"You have any trouble finding someone to stay with Davey?"

"He's doing a sleepover next door," she said defensively. "You can call if you don't believe me."

Oh, how he was tempted to do just that, but someone had to start the mutual respect and trust needed here, and it might as well be him.

"I believe you," he said, drawing a look of surprise.

"You do?"

"You're not going to lie to me about something you know I can check out for myself, Kelsey. I want to trust you. I always have."

"Yeah, right." She walked into the living room and tossed her fake fur jacket over the back of a chair, then looked around. "You haven't changed much."

Pete shrugged. "I didn't see any point to it. It's okay."

She frowned at that. "Just *okay* was always good enough for you, wasn't it?"

"And it was never good enough for you," he replied, regret, rather than accusation, in his voice. But even if he'd built his dream house while they were still together, it wouldn't have been enough. All she'd ever cared about was leaving for a more exciting life.

"I suppose that's true," she said. "Do you have any wine in the house? I could use a glass."

"You can't drink and then drive back to Richmond," he said.

She gave him a seductive smile. "Then I'll just have to crash here, won't I?"

"Kelsey!"

"Oh, don't go all weird on me, Pete. It's not as if we haven't slept under the same roof and in the same bed before. Maybe we should do that tonight, for old time's sake."

"I don't think so. What we had is over, Kelsey. Surely you know that by now. Hell, it was your idea to end it."

She ran a polished red nail down his cheek, then sashayed toward the kitchen. "Maybe I've changed my mind," she called over her shoulder as she apparently went in search of the wine she wanted.

Pete bit back a sigh. He was not going to let these seductive games of hers get in the way of the discussion they needed to have. If he overreacted and got her angry, they would wind up settling nothing. Besides, she was mostly talk.

She came back from the kitchen with two glasses of white wine and handed one to him. He set it aside.

"Let's talk about making peace," he said quietly. "For our son's sake."

Her expression brightened. "That's exactly what I'd hoped you'd say."

"You did?"

"It's time to put the past couple of years behind us, Pete. We can start over, make a home for our son." A smile touched the corners of her lips. "Maybe give him a baby brother or sister."

Pete stared at her. His mouth had gone dry, but he managed to squeak out one word. "What?"

"Don't look so shocked, sweetheart. We both know this is for the best. You believe in family. I've had my taste of freedom. It's past time for us to get back together and be the family Davey wants."

Pete shook off the panic crawling up his spine. "What exactly are you suggesting, Kelsey?"

"Darling, isn't it obvious? I want to move back home."

"You mean here, to town," he said, hoping he'd gotten it all wrong, though she was expressing herself pretty clearly for once.

She regarded him with tolerant amusement. "No, of course not. I mean right here, with you. This is our home, after all. Maybe we can even have that big wedding we missed out on the first time around."

The words hung in the air, leaving Pete speechless.

She put aside her own glass of wine and twined her arms around his neck, her breasts pressed against him. "Isn't that the news you've been waiting for all this time?" she asked, her face radiating confidence. "Davey and I are coming back to you."

Jo was going just a little stir-crazy waiting to hear from Pete. She knew they'd made plans for breakfast, but she wasn't sure she could wait till morning to find out what had happened when he saw Kelsey.

She sat at the kitchen table and watched the minutes tick off the clock. Each one felt as if it took an hour to pass. Surely the stupid clock was broken.

Since she didn't dare call Pete's and risk throwing a monkey wrench into whatever delicate negotiations were happening there, she called Ashley and announced, "I'm going out of my mind."

"Why? What's happened?" her sister asked at once. "Do you need me to come over?"

"No, I just need you to talk me down."

"Down from what?"

"This lonely limb I'm sitting on."

"You're talking in riddles. Stop it right this instant or I *will* come over."

Jo laughed. "I'm not literally on some limb."

"Thank God."

"Pete called Kelsey. She's supposed to be here now, so they can try to work out this mess."

"That's a good thing, isn't it?"

"It should be, assuming she'll listen to reason. I'm not convinced she will."

"I'm sure Pete can handle her," Ashley soothed. "He was married to her, after all. And if he can't, he has me as legal back-up. Based on what you've told me about her neglect, he has more than ample grounds to reopen the custody arrangement and file for permanent custody."

"He won't do that unless he has to," Jo reminded her.

"But it is a nice piece of leverage to have, don't you think?"

"I suppose. I just hate anything that turns Davey into a pawn between them."

"Which just proves that you're a better woman than his own mother."

"You're biased."

"Not about this," Ashley insisted. "The evidence

speaks for itself. You're putting the child's needs before your own. And just so you know, now that I understand the whole story, I have to admire Pete for doing the same thing seven years ago, even though it cost both of you very dearly."

"I know," Jo said softly. "Me, too. He's a good man, Ashley. I don't want to be the reason he or Davey gets hurt."

"Not you, sweetie. Kelsey will get full credit for that one, if she doesn't see reason. You didn't break them up. That happened long before you even came back to town."

"I suppose."

"Look, if you're so worried about what went on over there tonight, why don't you go on over?" Ashley suggested. "Pete probably figures you've crawled into bed by now and he doesn't want to wake you. There's no need to wait till morning."

Jo thought about that. "I suppose it wouldn't hurt. She'll be gone, so it's not as if I'll get her all stirred up again. If she's not gone, I'll turn around and leave. She'll never even know I was there."

"Sounds like a plan to me," Ashley enthused. "I hope Pete has good news for you when you get there."

"Me, too," Jo said with heartfelt yearning. "Me, too."

Pete stared at his ex-wife as if she'd suddenly grown two heads. "You want to move back home?" he echoed. "And get married again?"

Kelsey nodded. "Moving away, leaving you…" She shrugged. "It was a mistake, Pete. I want to try again. We belong together. We have a history. We have a son. I know this is what you want, too. You fought so hard to keep me from going. I finally get it now. You were right. What we have is too important to throw it all away."

"*You* threw it away, Kelsey. You can't just decide out of the blue that you want it all back. It's too late."

"It's never too late," she said, still clinging to him, her breath whispering against his cheek.

And then her mouth was on his, hot and urgent and demanding. Once the greediness of her kiss would have turned him on, but not now, not since he'd rediscovered what it was to like to be kissed with real love and passion, not just lust and convenience.

He tried to push her away, but she was determined. She cupped his head with her hands, ground her mouth against his until he tasted blood.

"Enough," he said, lifting her and setting her aside just as he heard a faint whisper of sound and a gasp. He whirled around just in time to see Jo's horrified expression before she took off at a run.

"Dammit to hell," he muttered, tearing after her, Kelsey and her ridiculous request forgotten. He would deal with her later. He wasn't going to allow her to ruin his one chance at happiness for a second time.

He caught up with Jo as she made the turn onto the main road. She was on foot, which must be why he hadn't heard her arrival. He fell into step beside her, but that only made her pick up her pace. She obviously wasn't going to make this easy, wasn't going to wait for explanations.

Finally he latched on to her arm. "Whoa, sweetheart, where are you going?"

Tears were streaking down her cheeks. "Home," she said fiercely. "Back to Boston." She frowned at him, then added bitterly, "Again."

"Why?" he asked, though he knew perfectly well that she was running because of what she'd heard Kelsey saying back at his house, what she'd seen. He couldn't be sure how much she'd heard, but it had evidently been enough. Too much, in fact.

"Because I won't stand between you and your family," she said, her voice cracking on a sob. She gave him a look filled with heartbreak. "We were so close this time, Pete, but I don't blame you for choosing them. It's what you have to do. They obviously need you."

He wanted to shake her gently, make her listen, but first he had to find the right words. Filled with desperation, he searched his heart.

Holding tight to her shoulders so she couldn't break away and run again, he said, "Look at me, Jo."

When she continued staring at the ground, he repeated, "Look at me. Please."

She finally lifted her gaze.

"Now listen to me," he pleaded. "Really listen, Jo."

He waited until she nodded, then said, "What I need is you," he said quietly, his gaze locked on hers. He couldn't get this wrong. He had to find the words to convince her to ignore whatever she'd seen and heard and listen to his heart. "It's you I need, Jo. Not Kelsey. It's always been you. I thought I was doing the honorable thing seven years ago, but all I did was make a bunch of people miserable. I won't do that again."

"But your son," she protested. "I know how much you love him. Kelsey's right. You should be a family, if at all possible."

"Davey will always be important to me. I'll never

abandon him, not for anyone, but it's over between me and Kelsey. Hell, it was over before it really began."

He brushed a wayward tear from her too-pale cheek. "You're the family I need, Jo. And we'll make a place for Davey, too, on whatever terms I can work out with Kelsey, but I won't give in to her emotional blackmail. I want to do things right this time. I want to marry you, if you'll have me. Maybe, depending on how things work out, Davey can spend more time with us, if you're willing, but Kelsey's out of the picture. She's my son's mother, but she is not the woman I love. Please," he whispered, "you have to listen to me. You have to *hear* me. Nothing I've ever said to you before was this important."

She was silent for so long, he thought he'd lost, but then a sigh shuddered through her and her eyes shimmered with a fresh batch of tears.

"Don't cry," he pleaded.

"Happy tears," she said, swiping at them impatiently. "Are you sure? Really sure?"

"That I want to marry you?"

She nodded.

He dug in his pocket and came out with several crumpled pieces of notepaper and a small velvet box. He tossed the notes on the ground, then flipped open the box to reveal a simple diamond set in platinum. "I bought this after I left your place earlier today. I'd planned on asking you in the morning, and I'd hoped to do it someplace a bit more romantic than a ditch by the highway," he said.

A smile trembled on her lips. "This is the most romantic place ever," she insisted. "The stars and moon are out, and I can hear the waves on the bay. What could be more amazing than that?"

He smiled. "I'm glad it's working for you. Do I get an answer?"

"I should make you wait," she said thoughtfully. Her eyes sparkled mischievously. "But I can't. I've been waiting way too long to hear those words cross your lips. Yes, Pete. Yes, I'll marry you."

He whooped, then spun her around until they were both half-dizzy. "You know, years ago, I thought maybe Rose Cottage was enchanted and that what happened with us there was some kind of dream, but it wasn't, was it?"

Jo shook her head and looked at the winking diamond on her finger. "No, the feelings were as real and lasting as it gets. It was only the humans who got it wrong for just a little while. Maybe we didn't believe hard enough. Something tells me, though, that the magic will be waiting when the next generation comes along."

"Darlin', there's no magic involved," Pete insisted. "I'm sure of that now. It's all about love. That old house has always been filled to bursting with it. A little bit was bound to rub off on anyone who passed through."

She gave him a sly grin. "Maybe I should loan it to Kelsey for a while. She needs to find a man of her own."

Pete laughed. "Something tells me she won't welcome any help from us."

Jo's expression sobered. "You need to go back and tell her, Pete."

He sighed. "I know, but can't I stay here for a couple more minutes and hold you?"

"A few more minutes," she agreed. "That's it. Then you have to go inside and make things right for your son. After that, you and I will have the rest of our lives to hold on to each other."

"That won't be nearly long enough for me," he said. "I'm holding out for eternity." He pressed a kiss against her lips. "Did you walk over here?"

"At this time of night? No way." She regarded him with chagrin. "I got so upset, I forgot all about my car."

"I'll walk you back to your car. Then I want you to go home and start a fire. Give me an hour and I'll join you. We have a lot to celebrate and we have a wedding to plan."

"Is it too much to hope that there will be more?" she asked wistfully.

Pete glanced at the house and knew the conversation awaiting him wouldn't be as easy as he wished it would be. "I hope so. She's not a bad person. She's just a little lost."

"Then show her the way," Jo said. She touched his cheek, her eyes shining. "And then come home to me."

"Ah, so you're thinking of Rose Cottage as home?"

Jo laughed and this time the sound was filled with mischief and joy. "Only till that house of yours is finished. And then I'm moving in before you change your mind and sell it to someone else."

"Never happen," Pete promised. "It was meant for you from the day I nailed the first boards into place."

"No," she said. "It was meant for *us*."

Epilogue

Jo's mother finally had time to plan a proper wedding. Jo and Pete had set the date for June in Boston and, to her mother's delight, in church, as Pete had gotten a religious annulment of his first marriage along with the divorce. Colleen D'Angelo was in her element making all the details come together. Jo hardly had to lift a finger, which was just as well since she was swamped with work in her new partnership with Mike. She'd been lucky to squeeze out a three-day weekend for the wedding and one night for a honeymoon. The real thing was going to have to be postponed for a while till things slowed down in both their lives.

She looked around the table at her family, all of whom had gathered for the rehearsal dinner, and felt contentment steal through her. Maybe it had always been meant to be this way. Maybe she and Pete had needed to endure a separation in order to know just how important this moment was.

She felt a tug on her arm and looked down at Davey. "What's up, sweet pea?" she asked.

He made a face. "Don't call me that."

She regarded him with exaggerated dismay. "Something's wrong with calling my new stepson sweet pea?"

"It's *dumb,*" he said emphatically. "It's what you'd call a girl."

"Oh?" she said, giving that serious thought. "Okay, then, want me to call you macho man?"

Davey's eyes lit up. "That's a good one. Yeah, you can call me that, but what do I call you?"

She heard genuine concern in his voice, which told her to take the question very seriously. "You've been calling me Jo. Do you think that should change?"

"I don't know. You're sort of going to be my mom now, so it seems like it should."

"I'm only going to be your mom some of the time," she reminded him. "Nothing changes between you and your real mom. She will always be the most important mom you have, and you're going to be living with her, same as always, just spending a little more time with your dad and me."

In fact, the visitation arrangements were only slightly more liberal than they had been before. Pete and Kelsey had worked out a revised plan, but at least Kelsey was sticking to them. Once she had finally accepted that Pete was going to marry Jo, she'd grasped the positive benefits of having a few more weekends to herself so she could make a new life, hopefully with a new man. Right now, though, she was using the extra time to take some college classes. She'd finally made peace with Pete's decision and started to think about what she could have, if only she worked for it. Maybe she'd eventually find that exciting life she'd always longed for.

"Still, you need a special name," Davey insisted, then grinned impishly.

That expression reminded Jo why she'd fallen in love with his father and with him. With the two of them there would always be unexpected surprises.

Davey gave her a triumphant look. "Maybe I'll call you sweet pea."

"I don't think so," she said, laughing. "Try again."

"But I can't think of anything," he complained, but then his expression brightened. "How about Mama Jo? Could I call you that?"

Tears stung Jo's eyes. "Nothing would make me happier," she told him, giving him a squeeze. "I love you, kiddo. I can't wait for tomorrow to marry your dad."

"Me, either," Pete said, leaning in to steal a kiss. "It's going to be the best wedding ever."

Jo met his gaze. "It's going to be my *only* wedding ever."

He stroked a finger down her cheek and regarded her solemnly. "Guaranteed, darlin'. Guaranteed."

The wedding was everything Jo had always dreamed about, everything she and Pete had talked about all those years ago. They were surrounded by her family and even Pete's uncle, who'd insisted on coming despite the arthritis that made it increasingly difficult for him to get around.

"Glad to see the two of you together finally," he told Jo right before the ceremony, when she paused to give him a kiss on her way to the altar. "It was too long coming. I knew way back that you were the best thing that could happen to this boy."

"I knew it, too," Pete said, giving him a wink right before he turned to stand by Jo's side in front of the priest.

When it came Jo's turn to say her vows, she looked deep into Pete's eyes and saw all the love that had been shining there when she'd first met him years ago. It had only deepened and matured thanks to everything they'd been through.

She touched his cheek. "I promise in front of our families and friends and in the sight of God to love you all the days of my life. I know that my Grandmother Lindsay is looking down on us today, and like your uncle, she's saying, 'It's about time.'"

"Past time," Pete said. He glanced heavenward. "I promise you that I will never let Jo down the way I did before." His gaze sought Jo's. "I make that same vow to you, to love you the way you deserve for all the rest of our days, to make a home with you, to share the joy of my son with you and to create a family of our own. I love you, Jo. Always have. Always will."

Jo's eyes stung with tears. There it was, the promise of eternity. And this time, she knew they wouldn't let anything tear them apart.

"Keep your eyes closed," Pete commanded.

"I've had 'em closed for what seems like hours. You blindfolded me in the car for the last two hours of the drive, which, I might add, you'll never get away with again. Where are we?" Jo grumbled.

"In a minute," he said. "Hold your horses."

She grinned. "Is that the way it's going to be now that we're married? You're going to be all bossy?"

He laughed. "Exactly how long do you think I'd get away with that?"

"Not long," she confirmed. "So when can I open my eyes?"

"When everything's ready."

"It's a hotel room. How much has to be done?"

To her increasing frustration, he ignored the question. She stood right where he'd set her down after carrying her across some threshold or another and waited, tapping her foot with mounting impatience.

"There," Pete said at last. "You can open your eyes now."

She scowled at him before she did. "It's a real tribute to my love for you that I have not peeked even once."

"It's a tribute to my faith in you that I knew you wouldn't," he retorted. "Do you want to discuss trust issues right now?"

"No," she said, then slowly opened her eyes to a room lit with candles and filled with bouquets of white flowers. French doors were opened to a sea breeze and the familiar sound of the bay gently splashing on the sandy beach. Delight washed over her. "It's our house. You brought us home. I had no idea it was ready."

"Didn't you wonder why I had you working so hard all over town? Mike and I taxed ourselves to come up with enough assignments that would keep you away from here. I didn't want you to know about this."

"I just thought Mike had made too many commitments and was really, really swamped," she said, moving slowly around the room in disbelief. He'd accomplished so much, and it was all exactly right. "It's beautiful, Pete. It's exactly the way I imagined it."

"I know you're not supposed to do a honeymoon quite like this, but I figured our first night together ought to be the place we were going to spend the rest of our lives. We'll make this house ours tonight."

He studied her intently. "I didn't do all the decorating. I just brought in enough furniture so we wouldn't be sitting or sleeping on the floor tonight. You can change it all, if you want."

"I'm not going to change a thing," she told him firmly. "We'll just add to it together, like the layers that come with time in a marriage."

He reached for her then. "I love you, Jo."

"And I love you." She met his gaze. "You know, I realized something while we were in Boston."

"What's that?"

"That this was the way it was meant to be. All the time apart was a blessing, because now we know how much being together really matters."

"That's one of the things I love most about you," he told her. "You've always been able to turn things around and find the blessings."

Jo wound her arms around his neck and rested her cheek against his. "And from now on, I won't have to look far."

He slid his arms around her. "You talking about the view?"

"That, and your face," she said quietly. "Being able

to wake up and look into your eyes is the greatest gift I've ever been given."

"Same here, darlin', and I'll never, ever take it for granted."

And like the tides changing just a few hundred feet away, Jo knew what they were feeling right now would go on forever, steady and reliable and powerful.

* * * * *

Please turn the page for a sneak peek
at the second book in Sherryl's
LOW COUNTRY TRILOGY,
Flirting with Disaster,
on sale in December 2005
from MIRA Books!

As interventions went, this one pretty much sucked. Not that Maggie knew a whole lot about interventions, having never been addicted to much of anything with the possible exception of making truly lousy choices in men. She was fairly certain, though, that having only three people sitting before her with anxious expressions—one of them the very man responsible for her current state of mind—was not the way this sort of thing ought to work.

Then again, Warren Blake, Ph.D., should know. He'd probably done hundreds of interventions for his alcohol- or drug-addicted clients. Hell, maybe he'd even done a few for women he'd dumped, like Maggie. Maybe that's how he'd built up his practice, the louse.

"Magnolia Forsythe, are you listening to a word we're

saying?" Dinah Davis Beaufort demanded impatiently, a worried frown etched on her otherwise perfect face.

Maggie regarded her best friend—her *former* best friend, she decided in that instant—with a scowl. "No." She didn't want to hear anything these three had to say. Every one of them had played a role in sending her into this depression. She doubted they had any expertise that would drag her out of it.

"I told you she was going to hate this," Cordell Beaufort said.

Of everyone there, Cord looked the most relaxed, the most normal, Maggie concluded. In fact, he had the audacity to give her a wink. Since he was yet another one of the reasons she was in this dark state of mind, she ignored the wink and concentrated on identifying all the escape routes from this room. Not that a woman should have to leave her own damn living room to get any peace. She ought to be able to kick the well-meaning intruders out, but she'd tried that and not a one of them had budged. Perhaps she ought to consider telling them whatever they wanted to hear so they'd go away.

"I don't care if she does hate it," Dinah said, her expression grim. "We have to convince her to stop moping around in this house. It's not healthy. She needs to get out and do something. This project of ours is perfect. If she doesn't want to help us with that, then she at least ought to remember that she has a business to run. She has a life to live."

"What life is that?" Maggie inquired with faint curiosity. "The one I had before Warren here decided I wasn't his type and dumped me two weeks before our wedding? Or the humiliating one I have now, facing all

my friends and trying to explain? Or perhaps you're referring to my pitiful and unsuccessful attempt to seduce
Cord before you waltzed back into town and claimed
him for yourself?"

Of all of them, only Warren had the grace to look chagrined. "Maggie, you know it would never have worked
with us," he explained with great patience. "I'm just the
one who had the courage to say it."

"Well, you picked a damn fine time to figure it out,"
she said. "What kind of psychologist are you that you
couldn't recognize something like our complete incom-
patibility a year before the wedding or even six months
before the wedding?"

Warren regarded her with an unblinking gaze. "We
were only engaged for a few weeks, Maggie. You were
the one who was in a rush to get married."

"I was in love with you!" she practically shouted, irritated by his determination to be logical when she was
an emotional wreck. "Why would I want to waste time
on a long engagement?"

Warren's patient expression never wavered. It was
one of the things she'd grown to hate about him. He
wouldn't fight with her.

"Maggie, as much as I would love to think that you
fell head over heels in love with me in a heartbeat, we
both know the rush was all about keeping up with Dinah
and Cord. The minute they got married, you started getting panicky. We'd already stopped seeing each other
after just a few mostly disastrous dates, but you decided
we should give it another chance."

"I was being open-minded," she countered. "Isn't
that what the sensible women you so admire do?"

Cord tried unsuccessfully to swallow a chuckle. Warren and Dinah frowned at him.

"I have to say, I think Warren is right," Dinah chimed in. "I think you latched on to Warren as if he were the last life-raft in the ocean."

"Oh, what do you know?" Maggie retorted. "You and Cord are so into each other, you barely know anyone else is around."

"We're here, aren't we?" Dinah asked calmly. "We know you're in trouble and we want to help."

"Who invited you?" Maggie responded sourly. "I don't need the three of you sitting here with these gloom-and-doom expressions on your faces trying to plan out my life. Hell, Dinah, you're the one who talked Warren into going out with me in the first place. Considering how things turned out, I should hate you for that."

In fact, she *was* pretty darn irritated about it. If it hadn't been for Dinah's meddling, Maggie would never in a million years have fallen—even half-heartedly—for a man like Warren Blake. He was rock-steady and dependable, quite a contrast to the men she'd always been attracted to in the past. Men like Cord Beaufort, as a matter of fact. Dark, dangerous and sexy.

If she were being totally honest, she'd have to admit that she'd known all along she was settling for someone safe with Warren. He might not rock her world, but he'd never hurt her either. At least that's how her muddled thinking had rationalized the relationship. As it turned out, she'd been wrong about that. He had hurt her, but mostly it was her pride he'd devastated, not her heart. If a man like Warren couldn't truly love her, who would?

That's what she'd been pondering inside her Charleston carriage house for a few weeks now. If she wasn't interesting enough, sexy enough, or lovable enough for Warren, then she might as well resign herself to spinsterhood. He was her last chance. Her safe bet. Sort of the way Bobby Beaufort, Cord's brother, had been Dinah's backup plan.

Even as Maggie was struck by that notion, she realized she should have seen the handwriting on the wall. Wasn't she the one who'd told Dinah that *safe* was never going to be enough? If it wasn't good enough for Dinah, why had Maggie ever thought it would work for her?

"Mind if I say something?" Cord asked, his gaze filled with surprising compassion.

Maggie shrugged. "Suit yourself."

"Here's the way I see it," Cord said.

He spoke in that slow, lazy drawl that had once sent goose bumps down Maggie's spine till she'd realized he'd never want anyone except Dinah.

"Nothing's stopping you from sitting in this house of yours all the livelong day, if that's what you want to do," Cord said. "Your art and antique gallery can pretty much run itself, thanks to those competent employees you've hired. And if it doesn't, so what? You've got a nice little trust fund from your daddy. You don't need to do a thing."

Maggie bristled. She'd never liked thinking of herself as the kind of spoiled little rich girl who didn't need to work for a living. She'd poured her heart and soul into making a go of Images, just to prove she was her own person. She'd never treated it like a hobby. She'd taken pride in the success of the high-end shop that catered as much to Charleston's wealthiest citizens as it did to the tourists who came through the historic district every day. As for her employees, she didn't know where Cord had gotten the crazy idea they were competent. She'd be lucky if they didn't run the place into bankruptcy.

If Cord was aware of her growing indignation, he ignored it.

"Maggie's a smart woman. I think we should let her decide for herself how she wants to spend her days," Cord continued mildly, aiming his words at Dinah and Warren and leaving Maggie to draw her own conclusions. "She can go back to work running her business, if that's what matters to her. She can come on out and help us with this project we've been telling her about and make a real difference in someone's life. Or she can sit right here and feel sorry for herself. It's her choice. I think once we clear out and give her some space, she'll make the right one."

Maggie saw the trap at once. If she did what she wanted to do and hung around here wallowing in self-pity and Häagen-Dazs ice cream, they'd worry, but they'd let her do it and they wouldn't think any less of her because they loved her. But in her heart, she'd see herself for the ridiculously self-indulgent idiot she was being. She'd lost a man. So what? Warren wasn't the first and undoubtedly he wouldn't be the last, despite her current vow to avoid all males from here to eternity.

"Tell me again about this stupid project," she said grudgingly.

Cord, bless his devious little heart, bit back a grin. "We're going to be building a house for someone who needs one. The church got the idea, a benefactor donated the land, and the preacher asked me to put together a volunteer crew. Dinah and her mama are in charge of raising money for whatever building supplies we can't get donated."

"What do you expect me to do?" Maggie asked suspiciously.

"What you're told," Dinah said with a glint of amusement in her eyes. "Same as me. It'll be a refreshing change for us. At least that's what Cord says. We'll be hammering and painting right alongside everyone else."

Maggie turned her gaze on Warren. "And you?"

"That's up to you," he replied. "I said I'd help, but I'll stay away if you want me to."

Maggie wasn't sure Warren had any essential skills for building a house, so sending him away might not be much of a loss, but why bother? Maybe it was time to show all of Charleston that she wasn't devastated by her broken engagement. It was past time she held her head up high and behaved like the strong woman she'd always considered herself to be.

"Do whatever you want to do," she said indifferently.

"Then you'll help?" Dinah asked.

"I'll help," Maggie agreed. "If I don't, who knows what sort of place you'll build. Everyone knows I'm the one with taste in this crowd."

"We're building a three-bedroom bungalow with the basic necessities for a single mom with three kids," Cord warned. "Not a mansion."

"You're building a house," Maggie retorted emphatically. "I'll turn it into a home."

But just as she said the words, Maggie spotted the satisfied glint in Dinah's eyes and wondered if she wasn't making the second worst mistake she'd made all day. The first had been opening the door to these three.

If you enjoyed what you just read,
then we've got an offer you can't resist!

Take 2 bestselling
love stories FREE!
Plus get a FREE surprise gift!

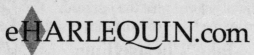

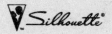

SPECIAL EDITION™

presents a new six-book continuity

MOST LIKELY TO...

Eleven students. One reunion.
And a secret that will change everyone's lives.

On sale July 2005

THE HOMECOMING
HERO RETURNS

(SE #1694)

by bestselling author

Joan Elliott Pickart

Former college jock David Westport was convinced he had it all—a beautiful wife, two wonderful kids and a good business in his North End neighborhood. Sandra Westport loved her husband dearly but was positive that he did have one regret—letting her sudden pregnancy derail his chances at a pro baseball career ten years ago. And when a college professor revealed a secret that threw all the good in David's life into shadow, Sandra feared her marriage was over. Could David rebuild his shattered dreams without losing the love of his life?

Don't miss this emotional story—only from Silhouette Books.

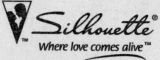

Where love comes alive™